Lucky wore n

The shoulder strap
Her fiery red hair f
curls. She'd brought a large metal spatula with her from the kitchen, and the way she held it seemed to indicate that if the need arose, she could use it for something other than turning food.

Colin's throat tightened as she leaned against the door, causing one of the straps to move so that her nipple peeked out. He stared at her intently. "Come here."

Her green eyes twinkled at him naughtily. "I would, but I'm afraid I might burn something."

"Baby, the only thing burning is me sitting here looking at you looking like that."

She slapped the spatula into her opposite palm, her gaze travelling in a leisurely way over his nude body where he sat on the bed. The action made him entertain all sorts of ideas.

"Over easy or sunny-side up?"

Colin allowed his mouth to curve into a slow, suggestive smile. "Any way I can get you."

Dear Reader,

In our first SLEEPING WITH SECRETS title, *Forbidden*, you met Leah Dubois Burger and bad-boy-to-the-bone JT West. And their relationship was really, really hot! But if you thought that was intense, just wait until you feel the chemistry between Colin McKenna and Lucky Clayborn!

In *Indecent*, sexy psychologist Colin refuses to take on provocative Lucky as a patient, namely because he wants to have sex with her in the worst way… Unfortunately, it's also in a way that's dangerous to his career. You see, this isn't the first time he's dealt with a patient's desire, and that episode is the reason he now handles only group appointments. But all too easily Lucky turns the tables on him, making him feel as if he's the one needing help. And with Lucky, he is…

Colin and Lucky's story is so unlike anything we've written before. We hope it proves to be one of those one-sitting reads for you! We'd love to hear what you think. Write to us at PO Box 12271, Toledo, OH 43612, USA, or at karayianni@aol.com. And be sure to visit us on the web at www.BlazeAuthors.com and www.ToriCarrington.com.

Here's wishing you love and hot, memorable reading,

Lori & Tony Karayianni
aka Tori Carrington

INDECENT

by

Tori Carrington

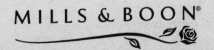

We wholeheartedly dedicate this book to Susan Till,
who reads between the lines and knows what we want to say
even when we don't. Thanks for making us look so good!

*First published in Great Britain 2005
by Harlequin Mills & Boon Limited,
Eton House, 18-24 Paradise Road, Richmond, Surrey TW9 1SR*

© Lori and Tony Karayianni 2004

ISBN 0 263 84451 X

14-0305

*Printed and bound in Spain
by Litografia Rosés S.A., Barcelona*

1

GOING WITHOUT sex wasn't Colin McKenna's idea of a good time. Which meant he'd had a pretty lousy time of it for the past three months.

His athletic shoes clapped against the cement walkway paralleling the Maumee River, his cadence even, the sound of his breathing filling his ears. To his right, the sun was just beginning to break the horizon causing the temperature to rise on the clear June day. He'd run this route along the river ever since buying his downtown penthouse condo last year. But in the past three months the route had lengthened and lengthened along with his rising level of sexual frustration.

Another man might take things into hand, literally.

Colin preferred running.

His lungs began burning, protesting the pressure he was putting on them. He grudgingly slowed his paced then came to a stop, panting as he turned toward the sun's rays and squinted out over the river to the East Side and International Park. He'd grown up here in Toledo, Ohio, though a long way from downtown in the suburb of Sylvania. But he hadn't hesitated when a block of newly renovated condos had gone up for sale in an old department store building, putting him in the heart of the midsize city that was an intriguing mix of old and new.

He took several deep breaths, each slower than the one before, as he brought his pulse rate under control. As a psychiatrist, he knew the power of mind over body. It was of some interest, then, that his body was increasingly overruling his mind's need for control.

He'd never paid much attention to the importance of sex in his life until he'd been falsely accused of indecent behavior by one of his patients three months ago. That was when his attorney had suggested he go without until the case was either dropped or settled in order to create a picture of himself as a model, upstanding citizen. Not that he hadn't been that before, but he realized he had been a serial dater.

The case was also the reason why he no longer counseled patients one-on-one but rather took only group and couples sessions.

Three hours, a shower and two such therapy

sessions later, Colin sat back in his office chair, listening as the married couple before him bickered about the price of their last meal out. Actually it didn't matter what the topic was, the couple would argue about it. How they'd managed to keep from killing each other much less stay married for the past ten years was beyond him.

Give up and head for divorce court now, he wanted to say, but didn't.

He glanced at his watch. Only five more minutes in the session to go.

Colin didn't think he'd last two.

He absently rubbed the back of his neck. There were times when being a couples therapist was just as bad as going without sex, if only because his experiences over the past ninety days seriously undermined his belief in the institution of marriage. There were two types of couples—married and unmarried—that came to counseling. With the first type, the union was beyond repair and they were looking for him to work miracles on it and with the second type the participants were genuinely interested in putting their individual needs aside for the greater good of the union.

More often than not he saw the former. And the extent of his job was to play referee. One of his three partners at the Sylvania Mental Wellness

Clinic had offered to get him scorecards for sessions like the one he was currently in the middle of or, better yet, a scoreboard and a buzzer to indicate when one of the spouses had entered foul territory.

In the case of the Hansens he would have ruled a TKO three sessions ago. Significant, considering this was their fourth session.

"Jocelyn," Colin said quietly, watching as the woman's face grew redder and spittle formed at the corners of her mouth. Normally an attractive woman, she looked like evil incarnate as she lit into her husband with all the finesse of a pro.

"...and if you think I'm just going to roll over and play patsy, you've got another think coming. I already have three kids. I don't need another. I work a full-time job, same as you, and if I'm too tired for sex every now and again..."

"Jocelyn," Colin said again, never having had to raise his voice during a session before but afraid this time might prove the exception.

Her husband, Larry, was shaking his head, his own color growing darker. "Shut up, Jos."

The room fell silent.

Colin blinked. It was the first time Larry had said something of that nature before. Normally quiet, he nodded and probably didn't pay attention to half of what was being said by either his wife or Colin. Not that Colin could blame him. Jocelyn didn't so much as speak with you as she spoke at you.

Colin took in Jocelyn's shocked appearance, spotting all the signs of a major outburst on the rise. He rubbed his thumb and forefinger against his closed eyelids. That was it. He was never getting married.

A brief knock on the door, then it opened. Colin frowned. The temporary receptionist that an employment agency had provided to fill in for their regular receptionist was not the brightest bulb in the string.

He squinted at the female figure that had come to a halt just inside his door. Definitely not the mousy temp he'd expected to see. Long, long legs encased in sheer black stockings. A short, short skirt that hugged her curvy hips in all the right places. A tight, tight white tank top that looked small enough to fit a six-year-old. Flame-red hair fell to the middle of her back and would no doubt tickle the dimples at the curve of her bottom when she was stripped down to her bare, creamy skin.

Mary Magdalene and the Virgin Mary all wrapped up in one provocative package.

His body was making it all too clear it didn't like his self-imposed temporary celibacy.

His mind told him to hold up on the decision never to marry.

"Ooops. Sorry," the walking advertisement for everything a man ever wanted in a woman said, then twisted her full lips. "Wrong room."

Colin lifted his pencil and pointed over his shoulder. "Rest rooms are the next door up."

She seemed to take her time as she sized him up, then smiled. "Thanks."

Such a simple word.

Such an unexpected reaction as his groin and his throat tightened farther.

The door closed and Colin reluctantly returned his attention to Jocelyn and Larry. Only Larry was still looking at the closed door, his tongue nearly lolling out of the side of his mouth. Meanwhile Jocelyn looked an inch away from smacking her hand against his chin and shearing his tongue in half with the help of his own teeth.

"My, look at that," Colin said before round ten of the Hansens' weekly boxing match could begin. "Our time is up."

He rose to his feet and put his notepad on the chair behind him. "I think we've made some good progress today,'' he lied. ''Same time next week?''

Jocelyn was still glaring at her husband while Larry shook Colin's hand and thanked him. Before they were even through the exit door on the other side of the office, Jocelyn had already begun her next verbal attack. Colin closed the door, hoping they didn't get into an accident on the way home. Not that he was particularly concerned about their well-being. Rather he was more worried about the unsuspecting drivers around them. Never mind the three children that waited at home.

As an only child of older parents, his upbringing differed greatly from what he guessed the Hansen children endured. Discussions at the McKenna dinner table had tended to evolve around page three of *The Wall Street Journal* or a novel one of them had recently read rather than whether his father's inappropriate appreciation of a woman's physical assets had been a shade beyond decent.

He edged around his desk and sat down. He wasn't cut out for this couples-counseling gig. He fared a little better at group therapy sessions— like the addictive personality disorder one that was on tap next, and the monthly sessions he sat

in on at a local runaway shelter—but still he preferred the one-on-one approach that allowed him
to make significant progress in a patient's psy-
chological development.

He made notes on the Hansens, put the file
aside, then pulled the five other files for the group
he was due to meet in ten minutes. He fingered
through them. He was familiar with four of the
members, but the fifth was new. He opened the
file on one Lucky Clayborn and sat back in his
chair. Court-ordered therapy for two D.U.I.'s in a
year and a half.

He pinched the bridge of his nose, silently
praying that Lucky Clayborn wasn't the woman
who had walked in during his previous session.

Unfortunately, the way his luck was running he
fully expected that the sexpot and the drunk driver
were one and the same.

FEW THINGS were hotter than a gorgeous guy who
had no idea how appealing he was.

Lucky Clayborn sat back in the soft leather
chair, her gaze focused on sexy Dr. Colin Mc-
Kenna while he listened to one of the other group
members.

As accidental as it may have appeared, her
walking into his office during his previous session

had been anything but. After getting no farther than Step Two in the Twelve Step Program on three previous occasions, she'd been curious as to what the court-approved Dr. Colin McKenna was all about. She wasn't an alcoholic, her court-appointed attorney had pointed out to the court during her last time in front of the judge. And while her word against the arresting officer's the second time around hadn't held much sway, she hadn't been drinking when she'd been charged with the last count—she'd been on cold medication. But it seemed ever since the lowering of the legal intoxication limit, a generous tablespoon of cold medicine before you got behind the wheel was enough to set off the Breathalyzer.

And if every now and again she liked to blur the edges of her life with alcohol, that was between her and the vodka bottle.

The problem was she hadn't gotten through the Twelve Step Program because she had, admittedly, been uncooperative. So the judge had restricted her driving privileges for six months and ordered her to six weeks of counseling (as an aside she'd also suggested Lucky stay away from any cold medications that contained alcohol).

So Lucky had wanted to get a look at the guy

who had the power to have her license taken away altogether.

And she'd liked what she'd seen.

She slowly recrossed her legs, watching the sexy doc's gaze slide to watch the movement even as he focused on the other patient's progress report.

"Miss Clayborn?" he said a moment later, startling her. "Would you like to go next?"

Go where? She almost asked.

Then she realized she was being asked to introduce herself.

She glanced over the four other group members—two men and two women—who had all shared their stories. Two admitted alcohol was their stimulent of choice while the other two claimed prescription drugs were to blame for their addictions.

She quietly cleared her throat then crossed her legs again. "I'm Lucky Clayborn and I'm here to get help for my habit of taking cold medication when I'm sick then getting behind the wheel of a car and going to work."

There was a heartbeat of silence, then one of the women laughed, the other three members smiled and Dr. Colin merely continued gazing at her with those rich dark-brown eyes without blinking.

"Cold medication was to blame for both counts?" he asked without consulting notes or a file or even looking away from her.

For the first time in a long time, Lucky broke a challenging gaze. "You've done your homework," she said quietly. "I'm impressed."

"And you're avoiding my question."

She folded her hands in her lap, trying to ignore how damp her palms were. "No. No, cold medication wasn't to blame for both counts."

She looked for something else to focus on rather than his face and found his hands an intriguing substitute. They were large and thick and it was all too easy to imagine them covering her breasts, her taut nipples between his thumbs and index fingers. Her gaze wandered up his perfectly starched white shirt and boring tie, resting briefly on the enticing, cleanly shaven stretch of his neck before lingering on his mouth.

After his bedroom eyes and thick, dark-blond hair, his mouth was by far his most appealing feature. She enjoyed watching his well-defined lips move when he said something in his deep baritone, then smiled. And he would undoubtedly know just what to do with his mouth when words were no longer the order of the day. Yes…Dr. Colin McKenna would definitely know how to kiss a woman. A man as attractive as he was not wearing a wedding ring—if she were married to him she'd probably solder it to his finger—didn't get far without tasting his share of women. And though she wasn't getting exactly the response she wanted from him with her leg-crossing, she did recognize the flare of attraction in his eyes before he covered it up and moved on to the next topic.

The problem was, he wasn't moving the topic anywhere at the moment. He'd stayed silent after her last comment, obviously expecting her to go on.

Lucky swallowed hard and shrugged. ''That's it.''

He squinted, as if trying to get a handle on her. She could have told him not to waste his time. There was no handle to find. If there was, she would have found it a long, long time ago and maybe wouldn't have to depend on that vodka bottle to help her get by every now and again when the shadows of the past grew long and her ability to battle them short.

Finally, Colin turned his attention to the man to his right.

Lucky shifted, though this time it had nothing to do with getting the sexy doc's attention. Rather she was slightly relieved that she no longer drew his attention. Of course she couldn't be sure if the tension filling her stomach had to do with his question or her insane attraction to him.

But she was sure she was going to find out....

2

COLIN COULDN'T REMEMBER a time when his tie
had felt tighter.

"Thank you, Dr. McKenna," Doris Borgdoff
said as she passed him on her way out the door.
Forty-five years old, mother of two grown boys,
secretary at Owen-Illinois, he found it interesting
that she still had trouble meeting his eyes when
she spoke. "I got a lot out of today's session."

Colin forced a smile and said something he
hoped was acceptable as his gaze shifted to the
final member of the group. The reason for the
peculiar tightness of his throat. The sole partici-
pant who had not participated, but who had ac-
complished what she'd set out to do, which was
to drive him to distraction.

Sexy Lucky Clayborn glided, rather than
walked, to stand in front of him and he was aware
of every inch of her shapely legs, her lithe body,
her full breasts under her thin shirt.

She smiled up at him, a seductive mixture of

fearless feline and mesmerizing minx. He wasn't even aware that she'd slid her hand against the door to close it until he heard the soft click of the catch hit home, essentially leaving them alone in his office.

"I was hoping to have a word…alone with you for a minute," she said quietly, her deep-green-eyed gaze trapping his.

Colin's tie was no longer tight, it was choking him. Everything that was male in him responded to everything that was female in her. A kind of primal reaction that elevated his heart rate and made him all too aware of how long he'd gone without sex.

And how much he wanted to have sex with her.

During the session he'd been overly aware of every move Lucky had made, the sound of her bare thighs sliding together as she crossed and recrossed her legs seeming to grow louder until he'd sworn he could smell the musk of her sex and had imagined what kind of underwear she had or didn't have on. His gaze dropped to her plump lips, devoid of anything but a hint of gloss and moisture from where she'd just licked them.

Dear God, she was a patient. And he'd had attractive patients before. Even attractive patients that had come on to him.

But no one had made his groin ache the way Lucky Clayborn did.

He broke eye contact and moved to stand behind his desk. The more distance between them the better. "What is it, Miss Clayborn?" he asked, pleased that his voice still sounded like his voice.

She stood still for a long moment, apparently considering his movements, then she crossed to the desk—behind, not in front—and smoothly sat on top of it, giving him a peek of hot-pink panties under the short black skirt.

"You call all the other patients by their first name," she didn't say so much as purr. "Why not me?"

She sat not a foot away from where he stood and he was certain now that he could smell her unique musk. An intriguing mix of ginger and one-hundred-percent turned-on woman.

"You're new," he managed to push past his tight throat. "I generally address new patients by their proper names until a doctor-patient relationship has had a chance to develop."

"Mmm." She slowly scooted over until she sat in front of him.

Despite his best intentions, Colin's gaze dropped to her sleek thighs, watching as her skirt hitched up a little farther. His mouth watered with the desire to put his tongue right there where a lone mole sat an inch or so away from the pink edge of her panties.

"Miss Clayborn," he said, trying to keep things light though he felt anything but. He met her gaze, noting the widening of her pupils, the unmistakable desire to be kissed tinting her alluring features. "It's my duty to remind you that as long as you're my patient, there can be nothing of a personal nature between us."

The way she was sitting directly in front of him, with her legs slightly spread, it would be all too easy to slide between those supple thighs, put his arms around her curvy body, then claim that decadent mouth of hers with a kiss that he knew would lead to so much more.

And boy did he want that. He wanted that bad.

She gave him a sexy half smile that suggested she knew exactly what he was thinking. "Shame," she whispered, though she stayed right where she was.

"Mmm," he admitted.

He forced his gaze away from her face, and his thoughts away from the voice that urged him to kiss her. Just once. Just touch his tongue to hers to see if she tasted as good as she looked. Slide his fingers up to see if her panties were damp.

"You didn't participate in the session much," he said, focusing on his Medical College of Ohio degree and his Ohio license to practice which hung in customized frames on the far wall. He'd worked hard to obtain both and wasn't about to throw them away because of one electrifying temptress. "I can't force you to, but you understand that I'm to submit progress reports to the court."

That seemed to urge her into action. She slowly slid from the desk, putting her luscious body flush up against his.

Making her all the more irresistible.

Colin froze, trying not to notice the way her hips pressed against his, the graze of her hardened nipples against his chest through her shirt and his. His erection pulsed and twitched. There was no doubt she was aware of his aroused state. Their physical closeness allowed for few secrets.

He didn't dare move. To do so would be to tip his hand, to let her know she had control. And he couldn't give that to her. To do so would be to undermine their professional affiliation.

To do so would be to lose control, period. Not just over his desires, but over his entire life. Because to kiss Lucky, with those false charges hanging over his head, would be akin to kissing his career goodbye.

"Well, we all do what we have to in the end, don't we?" she finally said.

She stepped away, but not before brushing against him in a way that made him grit his back teeth to keep from shuddering with need.

She smiled at him, picked up her purse from the desk, then let herself out the exit door.

Colin swallowed hard, and he was pretty sure sweat dotted his brow as he collapsed into his desk chair and made a mental note to himself never again to be alone in a room with Miss Lucky Clayborn.

LUCKY WAS LATE for work. Again.

Of course, it hadn't helped that she'd lingered at Dr. Colin McKenna's office after the group session, acting on an explosive attraction she hadn't felt in a long, long time.

She knew enough about men to know that not many of them had the strength to do what the sexy doc had. Oh, yes, involvement with her would very surely put his career in jeopardy. But she'd seen the fiery attraction in his eyes. Had felt his erection, long and thick, pressing against her sex.

And she'd known he had read her own signals clearly. Not that she'd been subtle about it. No, subtle would have been easy to ignore for a man like Colin McKenna. So she'd laid it out there for him…literally.

And he'd had the strength to refuse her when another guy would have shoved up her skirt and taken her right then and there on the desk.

A shiver ran the length of her spine as she rushed inside Harry's Sports Bar.

Lucky waved a quick hello to the head cashier as she hurried back to the employee lockers just to the right of the kitchen and then shoved her purse inside the one marked with her name. She was aware that a couple of the male waiters stood in the corner watching her strip down to her bra and shimmy into her Harry's T-shirt and apron. She barely glanced their way as she closed her tank inside the locker then twirled the attached combination lock.

"You're late."

The manager's name was Harry, although he wasn't the Harry on the sign, no matter how much he liked to pretend he was, especially when introducing himself to customers. "Hi, I'm Harry. Are you enjoying your meal?" he would say, leaving them to think he was the Harry of note.

He was somewhere in his mid-forties, was at least that many pounds overweight, and more often than not could do with a shower.

Lucky caught the way he stared at her breasts under the tight T-shirt and put her hand on her hip. "I told you I had an appointment."

"You also told me you'd make it here on time," he said to her breasts.

Since she'd landed the job four months ago, Harry had come on to her no fewer than ten times, usually when she worked closing and after all the staff had shared a wind-down beer. Now she usually opted for the earlier shifts even though the tips were better later, her patience for his unwanted attention wearing thin.

As she looked at him now, she suspected the same could be said for Harry. He looked a broken plate away from firing her and hiring another waitress that might be more open to his advances, despite the wedding ring on his left hand that he tried to hide with his class ring.

"I'm sorry. The session ran over," Lucky said then reached around him to pick up a tray so she could bus a table in her station nearby.

He caught her arm when she tried to pass. "Consider this your second warning, Lucky." He smiled at her in a way that made her skin crawl.

"I don't think I need to tell you there won't be a third."

"Understood," she said as Connie, another waitress, came up on Harry from behind. Since Connie had been there over a year, she was apparently more open to Harry's attentions.

She was glad when Harry moved his gaze from her breasts to Connie's, and she left to go clear the table and take an order from a couple of guys who were sliding into a booth near one of the big-screen televisions on the back wall.

Lucky had been waitressing since she was seventeen and the job was second nature to her. She liked the noisy atmosphere, the nonstop movement, the odd hours. If every now and again her feet felt swollen a point beyond pain and her back ached, she just treated herself to a long, hot bath and a day spent reading then rushed right back into the fray. She'd never given much consideration to doing anything else. She liked her life the way it was. Uncomplicated. Routine. Familiar. With a little spice like the delectable Dr. Colin McKenna thrown in to liven things up from time to time.

Just thinking of him made her smile.

"What'll it be?" she asked the next table as

she straightened the condiment caddy and took out her order pad.

She was doing pretty much the same thing an hour later when two men walked in and took a booth in the next station. She usually gave customers only a cursory glance, but one of the two warranted a double take. Simply because he was one unmistakable Dr. Colin McKenna.

Lucky stood staring in his direction. Of all the gin joints in all the towns in the world…of course, he would have chosen Connie's station to sit in.

"Are you going to take our order or not?" the guy in the booth next to her asked.

"Not," she said, walking away.

COLIN ACCEPTED a menu from the girl who had seated him and his best friend, Will Sexton, then stared at the five big-screen televisions on the walls tuned in to different sporting events. He raised a brow at an archery competition then settled his gaze on Will.

"Come here a lot?" he asked.

Will and he had roomed together in college and had remained best friends ever since. While he'd gone the psychiatric route, Will was now a surgeon at St. Vincent-Mercy's Trauma I Center.

"Don't you?" Will asked in his thick British

accent, cocking a grin at him. "Reminds me of the pubs back home."

Colin highly doubted that, but didn't say anything. Mirroring their choice in careers, Colin liked things quiet and subdued while Will's motto was the more chaotic the better. At least in most things. When it came to their sex lives Colin usually liked things a little more wild, while Will had always chosen the sorority girls with the pink ribbons in their hair. Even now he was dating a sweet little resident who planned to go into pediatrics.

Of course, Colin's preference had made turning down Lucky Clayborn in his office earlier all the more difficult.

Merely thinking of the hot, seductive woman made him tug at his collar, something he was free to do now that she was no longer in front of him.

"Welcome to Harry's, gentlemen. Can I get you something from the bar?"

Colin looked up and nearly choked for the second time that day when he found himself staring at none other than the woman in question.

As soon as he had verified that not only wasn't she a figment of his imagination, but that she was a waitress, he noticed that Lucky didn't look anywhere near surprised. In fact, her predatory smile told him she'd probably spotted him the moment he'd walked in.

"Hello, Dr. McKenna," she said with that sexy, throaty voice of hers. "Or may I call you Colin now that we're no longer in the office?"

Will raised a brow at him. "Friends, are we? And here I thought you'd avoid a place like this like the plague."

Colin dropped his hand from his tie. "Actually, we met elsewhere. Will, this is Lucky Clayborn."

Will briefly offered his hand to Lucky. "Such an auspicious name. Nice. Very nice."

Lucky stared at Will's hand for a long moment then finally put her own into it and gave a brief shake, apparently not used to the greeting. "Nice to meet you," she said, her gaze immediately returning to Colin.

He tried not to notice the way her T-shirt hugged her just as tightly as her tank had earlier, the green fabric making her eyes look huge in her pale face.

"Can I bring you a draft?" she asked. "Harry brews his own."

Colin swallowed hard and forced his gaze to his menu. "I'll have bottled water."

Will winked at her good-naturedly. "I'll take a

draft. Unlike the stuffed shirt here, I'm just knocking off work.''

Another waitress neared the table and stopped next to Lucky. Her whisper was none too subtle. ''What are you doing? This is my table.''

Lucky shrugged her away. ''Would you guys like to order now or would you like a few more minutes to go over the menu?''

Colin got the definite impression that if he so wanted, he could order her up with no problem.

His tie wasn't the only item of clothing that suddenly felt tight.

The other waitress strode away toward the back of the restaurant. Colin looked around Lucky to watch the other woman strike up a conversation with a man he guessed was the manager or the owner.

''We'll order now,'' he said, thinking the less interaction with Lucky the better.

''Are you in some sort of trouble?'' he asked after he and Will had made their choices.

Lucky glanced back to where the manager was staring at her while the waitress pointed in her direction.

She smiled as she accepted their menus. ''Nothing I can't handle.''

She walked away. As soon as she was out of

earshot, Will pulled at his own collar. "Did the temperature just get a little hotter in here or is it my imagination?"

Colin grimaced as he straightened his silverware. "It's your imagination."

"Well, I certainly hope so because I'm guessing she's a patient of yours. And you don't want to be taking any chances right now. Not with everything that's hanging in the balance." His gaze trailed back to Lucky. "That's one hot number, though. I don't know what I would do if a patient of her caliber came on to me the way she's coming on to you. A package like that has a way of making you forget about medical degrees. Pass her on to one of your colleagues quick, mate."

Colin had considered and discarded the option earlier. To pass her on to one of his partners wouldn't look good. And right now he couldn't afford even a hint of impropriety. "So why did you pass Miss Clayborn onto your partner?" he could hear himself being asked during a legal deposition. What would he say? "I wanted to screw her so bad my balls ached, that's why."

The sound of raised voices caught his attention. He looked over to where Lucky was facing off with the manager, the other waitress standing nearby with her arms crossed under her impressive chest. Colin couldn't make out what was being said, but given the man's stern expression he didn't think it was good.

And when Lucky took off her apron and then peeled off her T-shirt and draped both over the manager's head, he knew he'd guessed correctly.

There were hoots and hollers as Lucky strode, as casual as you please, toward the kitchen where she disappeared behind the doors.

"Whoa," Will said, his eyes wide. "Something tells me I won't be getting that ale any time soon."

Colin watched as Lucky came back out of the kitchen wearing the same tank she'd had on earlier. She ignored the manager as she walked through the place then out the front door.

He started to push from the table.

Will caught his arm, his expression stern. "I wouldn't if I were you, Col."

Colin considered him. "I know. But you're not me."

And then he went out after Lucky.

3

IT WAS raining.

Figured. Lucky kept her chin high and her shoulders back. It was raining in her professional life, so why shouldn't it be in reality?

She squelched a groan. She'd really needed that job. Aside from the good tips, the flexibility had allowed her to work around her morning job at the pancake house within walking distance of the bar. And considering that the pancake house didn't have an item on the menu that cost more than five dollars and ninety cents, her tips were minimal, by no means enough to live on.

And she'd thrown the job away for a man....

She tripped over her own feet, missing a puddle by millimeters. Had she ever done something so spontaneously irresponsible before? Not when it came to the opposite sex. Sure, she might like to shake things up a bit wherever she was, and she didn't take well to leering bosses, but a few unwanted stares at her breasts had never been enough for her to walk away from a well-paying job. And in this case, she had not only walked away from it, she'd gone to Colin's table knowing full well she'd be fired.

Of course, at the time it had seemed more than worth the unguarded expression on his face when he'd looked up to see her.

Now? Well, now she wondered which errant hormones had made her act so impulsively and how she might go about getting them back under control.

Sure, the shrink was thigh-quiveringly sexy. But no man was sexier than a good night's worth of tips. Not when she had bills to pay.

She opened the door of her twenty-five-year-old Chevy and slid onto the well-maintained leather driver's seat, breathing in the scent of old car and raspberry air freshener as she fished her keys from her purse. The ping of rain against the roof was the only sound…even after she turned the ignition key.

Not even a sputter, a whine or a crank from the old vehicle. Nothing.

Lucky tried starting the car again with the same results.

She rested her forehead against the cracked leather steering wheel and closed her eyes. Great.

Just what she needed considering she'd just lost her main source of income.

There was a light tap on her window. She leaned back to stare at the blurry image through the rain-spattered glass. Was that…

Colin.

"Are you all right?" she read his lips rather than heard the muffled words.

Lucky blinked at him. Was the doc really standing out in the rain with no protection, his hands tucked into his slacks pockets as he bent to look inside her car? Yes, he was. And in that one moment everything that had transpired in the past ten minutes had been worth it.

She yanked open the door and climbed out of the car to stand in front of him. He straightened, seeming to squint at her in the gloomy light.

"What was that you said?" she asked.

"I asked if you were all right."

Lucky twisted her lips, giving his tall, lean body a full once-over before returning her gaze to his eyes. "Considering I just got fired five minutes ago, my car won't start, and the lack of an umbrella has made my tank top transparent? I'm just peachy."

His gaze dropped down to her breasts. Lucky didn't have to look. It didn't take a physics professor to know that white cotton and steady rain made her look like a wet T-shirt contestant.

Only she was unprepared for the warm shiver that slaked through her at Colin's slow perusal.

She rounded him to stand at the front of her car. After sliding her fingers in between the grill slats, she tugged on the release then braced herself as she hauled open the old car's hood.

"You wouldn't happen to know anything about cars, would you, Dr. McKenna?" she asked.

He came to stand next to her, staring at the grease-covered engine. "I know enough."

"And would any of that knowledge help me out with what's happening now?"

He looked at her, his mind appearing to be on everything but the status of her car. "It's my guess your battery's dead."

He walked to the driver's door, opened it, then pushed in the button that turned off the headlights. When she'd gotten into her car, Lucky hadn't even been aware they were on. Then again, why would she? If the headlights had drained her sorry excuse for a battery, then there wouldn't be any juice left to illuminate them now, would there?

Great.

Colin closed the door then reached to close the hood.

Lucky turned to face him. The fact that they stood without a raincoat or an umbrella in the pouring rain didn't matter to her. Nor did it appear to matter to him as they stood just staring at each other.

"Well," she said slowly, feeling oddly turned on by the attention. Attention she had wanted only a few hours earlier in his office but that now seemed somehow…very intimate to her. "I guess you won't have to worry about running into me again here."

He nodded. "Fired?"

"Very."

His mouth turned up into a small smile. "How do you feel about that?"

Lucky narrowed her eyes. "Dr. McKenna, are you trying to psychoanalyze me in a parking lot in the middle of a thunderstorm?"

He looked up. "It would have to be thundering in order for it to be a thunderstorm."

Lucky could have sworn she'd heard a few cracks and felt the ground shake, but she wasn't going to say anything in case the sensations had nothing to do with the weather and everything to do with Colin McKenna.

"And you're avoiding my question," she said just as he had in his office earlier.

The very handsome Colin McKenna looked even more delectable mussed up and wet. "Sorry. Hazard of the trade, I guess."

"What is? That you always end up sounding like a doctor?"

He nodded. "Especially when talking to a patient."

That's right. They still were doctor and patient, weren't they? Despite all that had happened in her own life in the past half hour, their connection remained the same. A connection that prevented the more sexual one she wanted more in that minute than she had at any other point during the day.

"Mmm."

His smile widened. "Can I give you a lift?"

"What would your lunch companion have to say about your disappearance?"

He glanced back toward the sports bar.

Lucky reached into her car, took her keys from the ignition, and grabbed her purse. "That's all right, Dr. McKenna. I wouldn't want to ask you to do something that might appear inappropriate."

Actually, she wanted to ask him to do something very inappropriate. She wanted to ask him to kiss her. To brand her skin with his hands. To show her what she'd only felt earlier in the office when she'd provocatively brushed up against him.

"How will you get home?"

She took a card out of her purse and waved it at him. "It's called the bus."

Lucky began to round Colin to start toward Secor Road and the bus stop across the street, then stopped parallel to him. Despite the weather, she made out the warm scent of his cologne. Or was it aftershave? Whichever it was, the smell made her want to press her tongue to his skin to see if he tasted as good as he smelled.

And before she knew it, she turned to do exactly that.

COLIN HAD KNOWN a moment of disappointed relief when Lucky turned down his offer of a ride. He wasn't sure what he was thinking when he'd made the offer, but he knew it was linked to whatever had compelled him to come outside to see if she was all right.

And he needed to get a handle on it before he and the sexy waitress…patient crossed paths again.

He was pretty sure he exhaled when she began walking toward the road.

After a few steps, she stopped and turned. "Actually, there's one thing you can do for me real quick, Doc,'' Lucky said lightly grasping his arm. ''You can kiss me.''

Colin opened his mouth to protest. The problem was the movement allowed her better access as she took his bottom lip between her teeth, then kissed him like a woman who could teach classes on the subject.

He felt a groan grumble up from his chest. It had been a long, long time since he'd so thoroughly enjoyed a kiss. More than three months, though he'd gone without sex that long.

He stood still, reveling in the soft, uneven texture of her lips. The rasp of her tongue as she took full advantage and slid it past his teeth.

''Mmm.''

Lucky made that sound again that tugged on something within him. Something deep and elemental and undeniable.

He reached out to pull her closer when she pulled away.

Raindrops clung to her lashes, making them look longer and thicker and giving her cat-green eyes an even more vivid appearance. Whatever makeup she may have had on had long since been washed away by the rain, revealing a light smattering of freckles over her pale skin. And her red hair shone almost black with wetness.

"That was even better than I imagined," she said softly. "And I have quite an imagination."

Then she was walking away from him, her hips swaying, seeming completely oblivious to the rain and to him as she made her way toward the road some hundred yards away.

Colin absently rubbed his chin, then held out his hand, absently watching the rain pelt his skin then run off to accumulate in a puddle at his feet. He was soaked and somehow couldn't remember how he'd gotten that way. He glanced up toward the battle-gray sky then back to the street, only Lucky was long gone.

FOR AN ENTIRE WEEK Colin both dreaded and anticipated the moment when Lucky would walk through the door to his office and either prove or disprove his attraction toward her. A case of raging hormones, he'd tried telling himself over and over again. An instance of temporary insanity. But no matter how many times he tried to apply reason to the erotic kiss he'd shared with Lucky in that parking lot seven days ago, he fell well short of the mark.

Then the moment he'd been waiting seven long days for never came.

Colin sat back in his chair, tapping his pencil

against the incoming mail and files the practice secretary had placed on his desk after the group he'd finished with had vacated the room. The group that should have included Lucky.

He leaned forward, browsing through the files, looking for hers. Normal procedure dictated he contact the court, let them know the terms of their orders were being violated. But he was reluctant to do that. Maybe she'd got caught up at work. Perhaps she hadn't repaired her car.

He couldn't find her file.

Grimacing, he went through the pile again with the same results. A pink envelope fluttered from the files in his hands and landed squarely in the middle of his lap.

That's odd. It looked like expensive personal stationary. Definitely not the type of thing he would think of Lucky possessing. He slit open the side with his opener and took out the single sheet of pink paper.

She's pretty. I could have been pretty for you.

Colin's blood ran cold.

While the handwriting wasn't familiar, the words—or rather the taunt in them—was.

Jamie Polson.

He pushed from his chair and didn't stop moving until he stood in front of his secretary's desk.

Having been out with the flu the week before, Annette looked the worse for wear.

"Where did this come from?" he asked, flashing her the envelope that simply said Colin across it.

Annette blinked at him. "I don't know. I don't remember seeing it when I sorted through your things a little while ago." She took the envelope and turned it over. "This I definitely would have remembered." She smiled as she handed it back. "Love letter?"

Far from it, he wanted to say.

"Hi," the breathless greeting sounded behind him.

Colin turned to find Lucky Clayborn smiling at him sexily. He nearly crumpled the letter and envelope in his grip. Someone had gained access to his office to put Jamie's card there. And the card itself bore an unspoken threat of sorts that upped the level of tension. He'd hoped time would allow Jamie the space to move on. To drop the case.

Instead Jamie appeared even more determined to keep him on the run, both in court and out. And he couldn't help wondering at the coincidence of Lucky's presence at the same time he'd discovered the card.

Colin discovered he was staring at Lucky's full mouth and allowed his gaze to linger there before lifting it to her eyes. "You're late," he told her. "The session's over." He stared at his secretary. "Where's Miss Clayborn's file?"

Annette appeared puzzled as she answered the phone then put someone on hold. "In with Dr. Szymanski's files, of course. Miss Clayborn called and asked to be transferred last week."

Lucky had moved to Morgan Szymanski, one of his partners?

Colin's pulse rate leapt at the knowledge that Lucky was no longer his patient.

"Do you have a few minutes?"

Lucky had asked the question from behind him, but Colin didn't trust himself to look at her. Without the doctor-patient wall standing between them, there was no longer any reason to resist her. He stared at the note in his hands then glanced at her.

"Why don't we talk in my office?" he suggested.

4

BEING INSIDE Colin's office with him, alone, was exactly what Lucky had had in mind.

She followed the handsome doc through the door to the right of the secretary's desk, waiting until he closed the thick wood before she did what she'd been yearning to do all week.

She stepped within breathing distance and kissed him fully on the mouth.

Incredible…

Lucky had just spent the past hour getting to know her new therapist and her three new group mates. She'd volunteered more than during last week's session, though Dr. Szymanski had been even less impressed with her participation than Colin had. But, with the simple touch of her lips against Colin's, she forgot all about the fact that she was to begin keeping a daily journal. Gone was her agitation at her inability to find a job. A distant memory was the dent to her savings made by the money she'd had to pay to replace her car battery.

And long forgotten was her fear that Colin would refuse to see her even though she was no longer his patient.

Instead she just…well, she merely allowed herself to feel.

As she lifted her hands to thread her sensitized fingers through his velvet hair and intensify the kiss, sizzling heat spread across her skin, then went deeper, igniting her nerve endings in a flash fire. Want pooled in her belly, tension coiling even though her muscles relaxed.

There was something about this one moment in time that made the world look different to her somehow, the instant when she gave herself over to attraction and allowed her body to lead instead of her mind. There was something primal in the action, something freeing.

Something that freed her from her past, if only for a short while.

Kissing Dr. Colin McKenna did all that and much, much more.

By now Lucky should have dived for the waist of his pants, seeking even greater release. Strangely she seemed to be satisfied merely kissing the handsome doc. She couldn't remember feeling that way before—happy simply feeling the firmness of a man's lips against hers. Usually her mind had already moved ahead a step and her hands and body quickly followed. Now it seemed to take every ounce of concentration to kiss him.

Colin groaned and backed her toward the leather couch positioned against the wall under a print of downtown Toledo. The same couch Lucky had fantasized about taking him on a week ago. Regaining some control over her actions, she turned him around so she could push him down against the rich, fragrant leather. The instant he was prone she climbed on top of him, mindless of the way her miniskirt hiked up her thighs, focused only on the red-hot sensations flowing through her.

It felt so good, so right, so natural to be doing what she was. Colin cupped her breasts and she gasped, surprised by the shock of his touch. He broke the kiss and gazed down at her chest as he stroked her through her cotton top. But she could do him one better. She reached for the hem and hauled the material up and over her head, leaving only her red lace demi-cup bra behind.

She hungrily licked her lips as she watched the brown of Colin's eyes nearly disappear under his dilating pupils. She began to bend to kiss him again, but the feel of his fingertip burrowing into the top of her bra then rasping against her distended nipple stopped her. She watched, trembling, as he peeled the lace back from her breast then lifted his head to suckle her deep into his mouth.

Lucky stiffened, her womanhood pulsing between her thighs, her heart thudding against the wall of her chest. She'd rarely experienced such a burning need to have sex with someone before. Oh, she'd always loved sex. But the hungry heat accumulating low in her belly took her breath away.

She wriggled her hips, happy when the thick ridge of his hard-on fell between the sides of her fleshy valley. She stretched her neck, riding out the waves of sheer pleasure at the meeting, despite the obstacle of their clothes.

Colin took advantage of the momentary lowering of her barriers to reverse their positions so that her back was against the soft leather and he pressed against her front. Lucky stared up at him in part surprise, part wonder, but most of all need.

When he leaned to kiss her, he did so with animal abandon. He bit and sucked and plucked, his breathing ragged, his hips cradled hard between her thighs. Lucky blindly pulled at his shirt, tugging it from his pants, then flattened her hands against the solid plane of his abdomen. He was rock-hard and lean and so hot she nearly singed her palms. She pinched his flat nipples, listening to the low growl in his chest, then dove for his pants, the sound of his zipper opening loud in the otherwise quiet room. She knew such an urgency to have him inside her that when she felt his finger edge inside the elastic of her panties and flutter against her clit, she nearly came on the spot.

Finally Colin's throbbing erection filled her hand. Lucky pulled back from their kiss so she could see the thick width and length of him. Her doing so seemed to turn him on even further, his hips bucking involuntarily. She gently squeezed, then moved her hand up the shaft without releasing her grip, watching moisture gather on the tip.

Colin shuddered against her at the same time he thrust two fingers deep inside her dripping wetness. The move was so unexpected that Lucky reached orgasm, bearing down on his hand and gyrating as sensation after sensation crashed over her.

Then the hand was gone from between her legs and was instead clutching her jaw. She blinked open her eyes. But rather than see the man who had given her the best orgasm she'd had in a very long time, she saw Colin's angry face.

''Did Jamie put you up to this?'' he ground out.

ONE MOMENT Colin had been on the verge of spilling his seed all over Lucky's hand, the next he was seeing her as the enemy, a modern-day Mata Hari bent on destroying him.

He glimpsed the fear in Lucky's eyes before she quickly blinked it away.

Colin cursed loudly and rolled off her luscious body to stand. He slipped his painfully erect penis into his pants, then tucked his shirt in and did up his pants.

''How much did Jamie pay you?'' he said after long moments.

Lucky was right where he'd left her, her fingers gingerly tracing the line of her jaw where he'd gripped her, perhaps a little too hard.

She swung her legs over the side of the couch, and tucked her breasts back into her bra. Her golden-red hair was sexily tousled, her color high. And Colin had no idea how he'd found the strength to deny his need to have sex with her.

''What in the hell are you talking about?'' she finally asked, pulling her top back over her head then removing her long hair from the back. "And who in the hell is Jamie?"

Colin rounded his desk. A good fifteen feet separated him from the woman he'd nearly ravished mere minutes ago, but it might as well have been nothing. His nose was still filled with her musky scent. His body still ached with the desire to claim her. "Come off it. A guy doesn't get this lucky unless he's going to pay for it later."

She flicked him a fiery smile. "Yes, well, this Lucky doesn't do it for money."

She got up from the couch and straightened her short skirt.

Colin crossed his arms. "The timing of your being assigned to me…your coming on to me so hard…switching doctors then showing up here…it has to be more than coincidence."

She stepped toward his desk, making his pulse leap. "Whoever this Jamie is, she really screwed you up, huh?"

Colin found it more than a bit odd that he was standing in his office with a patient—ex-patient— and she was the one doing the analyzing.

"I consider myself a little on the suspicious side, but you," she was standing in front of him now and poked her finger into his chest, "you really take the cake, Dr. McKenna."

Colin stared into her flushed face for long moments. Could he be wrong? Could everything that had happened between him and Lucky have been just a natural progression of events?

Even as he asked himself the question, he knew there was nothing natural about his wanting to claim her in a way he'd never claimed another woman before. Or perhaps it was purely natural, some kind of primal instinct to overpower his enemy.

She tsked as she ran her fingertip down over his buttons. "It's a shame."

She turned around and walked toward the exit door.

"What is?" Colin couldn't resist asking.

"That I won't be seeing you again." She opened the door, then stood leaning against it. "You see, I make it a habit not to get involved with anyone more screwed up than I am. And you, Colin, have demons not even I can compete with."

He squinted at her as she gave him a once-over.

"It really is a shame. I have the feeling you're very good in the sack. And I definitely was interested in finding out how good."

Colin winced at the quiet click of the door closing.

FIVE DAYS LATER Colin was no closer to finding out the truth behind what had happened than he had been when he'd been cushioned between Lucky's sweet thighs, literally an inch away from having sex with her.

"Come on, Mac, get your game on!"

Colin absently twirled the tennis racket in his hand and stared across the tennis court at Will who had just taken the first set and was two points into winning the next game.

The ball hit the center line then whizzed right by his left ear.

He'd agreed to meet his friend at his condo complex for tennis hoping some exercise and Will's company would help him forget about what had transpired in his office. Instead all he could think about was that it was Saturday morning and he had two whole days to fill before he could go back to work on Monday morning. Two yawning spring days that he usually looked forward to but now dreaded.

Twenty minutes later Will called the second set and tossed him a clean towel as they left the courts.

Will grinned at him. "Well, that was certainly a nice change of events. You usually beat the crap out of me at tennis."

Colin used the towel to wipe his face, though he didn't need it, then draped the terry cloth around his neck. "Yeah, well, I took pity on you this morning."

Will nudged him in the arm with his covered racket. "No, mate, you're distracted. And I don't think it's one of your whackos behind this one."

Colin grimaced at his friend. "For a doctor you can be very insensitive."

"Me? What would make you say that?"

"Whackos?"

"I'd never call them that to their faces."

"Your referring to them that way at all makes you insensitive."

Will chuckled. "I'll let you have that one. If only because I'm concerned about your mental welfare after this morning's match."

They walked in silence, winding around the three buildings that separated the tennis courts from the Victorian block that held Will's condo. Will made some comments about the quality of the women sunbathing at the pool then turned his attention back to Colin.

"So, are you going to share who she is or not?"

"Who?"

''The wily female who's stolen your brain straight out of your head.''

''There's no one in my life right now. You know that.''

''I know that's what your attorney advised.''

Colin slanted him a wary look.

''Good, then. You wouldn't mind doubling with me and Janet then tonight.''

''What?''

''You heard me.'' Will feigned a couple of tennis moves then continued walking next to him again. ''The pretty resident has finally agreed to go out with me, but only on the condition that I bring someone along for her girlfriend.''

''No way. If you'll remember correctly, my attorney advised me not to date anyone.''

''This won't be a date. This will be two pals getting together and running into a couple of girls while they're out.''

''Mmm.''

''You wouldn't deny a guy a chance to take the pretty pink ribbon out of Janet's hair now, would you?''

That's how Will always referred to the women he dated. And quite accurately at that. While it was highly unlikely Janet wore an actual pink ribbon, she was the type that would have done so in high school. While she was the head varsity cheerleader.

"I would and I am."

Will took his keys out of his pocket as they neared his building. "Why? Has something happened on the Jamie front I don't know about?"

Colin ran his hand over his face, not really up to talking about it just then. "Yeah, a couple things. But nothing to be worried about."

Will held open the door for him, but when Colin would have entered, two young women bounded out, looking as if the only thing they would do with pink ribbons was tie them around their body piercings. Short, tight T-shirts and even shorter denim cutoffs revealed bodies buff enough for the cover of *Playboy* without the need for airbrushing.

"Hi, Willy," the short brunette said, stopping in front of Will and smiling at him in open suggestion. "So when are we going to hook up? How about tonight?"

Colin covered his grin with a none-too-discreet cough while Will squirmed under the sex kitten's attentions. "Another time, perhaps?"

"Mmm. Another time. I'm going to hold you to that, Willy."

The woman gave Will a loud kiss then followed

after her friend who was a good twenty feet down the walk.

"Friend of yours?" Colin asked.

"Neighbors." Colin followed Will's line of sight. Yes. Despite his preference for young and innocent, Will's gaze was definitely glued to the brunette's pert backside.

And what a backside it was, too.

"And she's gay."

"Is not," Colin objected.

"Is, too. That's her girlfriend. And when I say girlfriend, I don't mean they're both girls and they're friends. I mean they share the same bed at night and they do more than sleep in it. Come on. Maybe it will be quiet now without the two of them playing their music so loudly."

Colin led the way inside and climbed the steps to the first floor where Will's condo was located. Halfway up, Will stopped and said, "Don't tell me it's the girl from the bar that's got you all worked up."

Colin turned to stare at his friend. "What?"

Where in the hell had that come from?

Will jabbed a thumb over his shoulder. "It's just that I was thinking about how those two were just your type—well, if they went in for that sort of thing, anyway—when I remembered that girl, that redhead that got fired from the bar.''

Colin looked away.

"All this, your distracted state, it is about her, isn't it?''

Colin cleared his throat. "Are we going to catch a shower and get going to that lunch at the club or not?''

Will slowly ascended the stairs to stand next to him. "Oh my God. I'm right, aren't I? You're preoccupied with thoughts of banging a patient. An out-and-out whacko.''

"She's no longer my patient. And she's not a whacko.''

"Oh? Cured that fast, hey?''

Colin stared at him, then at what Will was staring at. Namely, the fist Colin had raised.

Colin blinked. He'd never been a scrapper. Had never even gotten into a fistfight. Not in elementary school. Not in junior high. Never.

So what did it mean that he had a fist raised against his best friend?

"Whoa. This is worse than even I feared,'' Will said quietly as Colin regained control of his hands and his thoughts. "I have some advice for you, mate,'' Will said as he unlocked his condo door then led the way inside.

Colin tensed at the blast of cold air that hit him. He hadn't turned on the air conditioner in his own apartment, although they'd had it on at the office for a few weeks now.

"And that is?"

Will put his tennis gear away in the hall closet then turned to grin at him. "Come out with me tonight. I bet Janet's friend will be able to make you forget what's-her-name."

That's what *he* thought.

"Or else…"

Colin sat down on the white leather couch. Everything in Will's place was either white or off-white. Well, there was no accounting for taste. He and Will didn't share the same taste in furniture or women.

"Or else what?" he prompted when Will didn't immediately offer.

"Or else screw the woman's head off and get her the hell out of your system."

5

"ANNETTE, could you please bring me Miss Clayborn's contact information?"

Two days later Colin sat tensely in his office chair. It was five before five and the staff was about to go home. But the lateness of the day and his own uncomfortable interest in the sexy siren wasn't what prompted his request for Lucky's file. Rather, his partner Morgan Szymanski had just left his office after consulting with him on what to do about Lucky's not showing for her group session that afternoon.

A brief knock then the door opened and Annette handed him a paper. "Just put it on my desk when I'm done, okay? I'm on my way out."

Colin thanked her and wished her a good night as he stared at the sheet sitting in the middle of his desk.

So innocuous.

So dangerous.

He'd managed to talk Morgan out of contacting

the court, although even now he couldn't be sure why. He supposed after what he'd done last week, he owed Lucky at least the benefit of the doubt. After all, she had shown up for her previous two sessions.

And, after all, he had practically bruised her jaw when he'd accused her of being sent by Jamie.

He blew out a deep breath then leaned back in his chair and picked up the paper. Home phone, address, the works. Colin eyed it, familiar with the northwest Toledo area near the Michigan line, though he'd never been there.

He picked up the phone, then put it back down, cursing under his breath.

In the two weeks since he'd met Lucky Clayborn nothing about his life had seemed right. If he wasn't thinking about her, he was ordering himself not to think about her. And when he did allow himself the luxury of remembering her, he got hard as a rock, recalling how she'd opened her thighs to him, and how her pale fingers had squeezed his erection.

Colin clamped his eyes closed, trying to banish the thoughts.

He'd met with his attorney yesterday, but his father's old friend Don Maddox was no closer to settling the fraudulent case against Colin than he'd been three months ago.

Meanwhile Jamie was making it clear that Colin's life was an open book.

From notes left on his car, to curious answering machine messages, whenever Colin began to forget about Jamie's presence, he was reminded again that out there somewhere someone had it in for him.

He'd taken the notes and made copies for his attorney, but at this point there was no solid way to connect Jamie to the goings-on. Besides, the police likely wouldn't be interested unless and until a real physical threat was made.

Colin ran his hand through his hair several times. Wasn't the threat to his career enough?

He grabbed a yellow legal pad, scribbled Lucky's home address near the bottom, then ripped the slip off and stuffed it into his pants pocket. No matter what was happening with the case with Jamie, he was worried about Lucky. There was…something about her that called to him on a level he had yet to understand. Despite her ballsy behavior and saucy smiles, he was concerned about her in a way that had nothing to do with sex and everything to do with her.

But to initiate contact with her outside the of-

fice to inquire about office matters was like inviting the devil to come out to play.

He grabbed his jacket, then locked his office
door after himself.

Devil or not, he needed to see that she was
okay.

*Screw the woman's head off and get her the
hell out of your system.*

Will's direct words of advice ran through his
mind. He put Lucky's contact info on Annette's
desk, leafed through his phone messages, then
headed for the parking lot. As crude as it seemed,
his best friend might have had a point. Colin was
all too aware that the more you made an object
off limits, the more appealing it became. Was that
what was happening with him and his growing
obsession with Lucky? First she'd been inacces-
sible to him because she'd been a patient. Second…well, second, he'd allowed paranoia to get
the better of him, although if he'd been thinking
clearly he would never have allowed things to go
as far as they had last week. When he'd invited
her into his office to talk about her having
switched doctors, he'd been fool enough to believe he could control his sexual impulses. What
he hadn't anticipated was Lucky taking the initia-

tive and kissing him, putting him at a very definite disadvantage.

He pressed the button on his key chain to unlock his Lincoln Navigator SUV then climbed inside the sleek black-and-tan vehicle. And what made him think he'd be any better at controlling what happened if he showed up unannounced at her house?

He caught sight of his reflection in the rearview mirror and grimaced. He looked tired even to himself. And this constant obsessing about Lucky wasn't getting him anywhere. Whatever the outcome of this visit, he needed to attain some kind of mental closure. If he and Lucky had sex…a long, hot shudder ran through his body. If he and Lucky had sex, well, they were adults and consenting.

If they didn't, he hoped that whatever transpired would be enough to stop her from haunting his dreams at night. From interfering with his work during the day when thoughts of her crossing and uncrossing her shapely legs intruded. From compelling him to seek her out outside office hours on a Monday night.

He pointed his car in the direction of her apartment and pushed the button to roll down the window rather than switching on the air-conditioning.

All around him were the unmistakable signs of summer. Convertibles roared by, stereos pumping out thick, bass-heavy music. Kids played on neighborhood streets. The ice-cream parlors were open for business and full of Little League teams sitting at picnic tables eating cones either as a reward for winning or as consolation for losing.

The scenery was familiar, yet it seemed odd to Colin that while he wasn't looking the season had changed. Though it had been rainy and chilly only two weeks ago when Lucky had first walked through his door, now summer was in full swing, as were the colorful activities that went along with it. And the sensory input was almost overwhelming. When he ran early in the morning, just before dawn, most of the city was still asleep, the warming temperatures and changing vegetation the only reminders of the time of year. There were no children learning how to ride a bike for the first time. No young women in cut-off shorts. No cars cruising by blaring rap music. There was only him and the river and the odd jogger or two.

He rolled the window back up then switched on his own state-of-the-art radio to an oldies station. The song "Summertime" filled the interior of the SUV. He immediately changed the station to classical, looking for something to drown out the sounds of summer around him, but mostly hoping for something to calm his growing anticipation of seeing Lucky again.

He pulled his collar away from his throat, surprised to find he was lightly sweating, although it was relatively cool in the car. And if he checked his pulse, he was sure it would be a couple of beats above par for him.

He'd been engaged once. A long time ago. He'd just graduated from medical school and had completed his residency at the Medical College of Ohio, and he'd figured what the heck? He'd been dating Amanda on and off—but mostly on—for the past three years. The next logical step was marriage, right?

Wrong. Oh, she'd accepted the two-carat engagement ring. And they'd picked out wedding invitations and shopped around for houses together. They'd seemed perfectly matched. He was a psychiatrist. She was a lawyer. They would easily gross well into six figures annually. Enough to start a family, live anywhere they chose. They weren't limited by resources in any way.

But their sex life…

Colin absently rubbed the back of his neck.

His sex life with Amanda had been perfunctory at best right from the beginning. While they'd

matched up in every other area of their lives—
they traveled in the same circles, laughed at the
same jokes, were both early risers and joggers,
enjoyed going to the same restaurants and films
and exhibitions—in bed she stopped short of staring at the clock on the night table, and he always
felt rushed to finish. Afterward as she snuggled
close to him, seeming to prefer his embrace more
than his lovemaking, he'd felt oddly…empty. Un-
satisfied.

And the closer the wedding got, the more un-
satisfied he'd become.

Then one night, after a particularly aggravating
sigh of impatience from Amanda during sex, he'd
rolled off her without climaxing and asked her
what was wrong. She'd assured him nothing was
the matter, that she enjoyed making love with him
and then she'd tried to coax him into continuing.
But he'd put the brakes on and after a long, awkward silence had suggested they postpone their
wedding plans and consult a therapist.

Amanda had been horrified and suggested that
maybe they shouldn't marry at all.

He'd agreed and the next day life had gone on
as if she'd never been a part of it.

After seven years of higher education and another seven of work experience, Colin still men-

tally debated what had happened between him and Amanda. He'd thought he'd loved her. To this day he still cared about what happened to her, and he'd even attended her wedding five years ago to an old classmate of his from way back. They have two children now. Surely if he had loved her he would feel something other than happiness for her? Wouldn't jealousy be mixed in there somewhere? Pain? Or had his love for her been the same kind one sibling would have for another?

Was romantic love really love without strong sexual chemistry between the two participants?

And was great sex without love enough to see a couple through the years ahead?

He supposed his experience with Amanda was one reason he was attracted to more sexually available women. Not to say that every woman who wore her blouse buttoned to the neck was asexual. But in his experience over the past few years, most women who wore clingy miniskirts and tight shirts that sexily displayed their physical assets were strongly sexual. And it seemed he still craved that accessibility.

If he needed any more proof of that, he need note that he was sitting in the rutted gravel driveway of Lucky's residence.

The first thing that registered was how beaten

down the structure looked. Not just the house itself but everything around it. A free-standing garage was off to the right at the end of the gravel driveway, the windows in the doors broken and cracked and grimy, half the shingles missing, and the roof itself leaning in a way that indicated it wasn't going to be standing much longer.

The same description could fit the one-story house. Putrid green, the peeling paint barely covered the warped wood exterior and he could make out where an addition had been poorly built on, the newer half covered in oxidized white aluminum siding. The small front porch was filled with stuffed black garbage bags, while a simple, faded American flag sticker was attached to the inside of one of the windows. Abandoned tires and car parts littered the overgrown grass of the lawn, the wildflowers sprinkled throughout doing precious little to improve the appearance.

Colin slowly climbed from his SUV, squinting against the evening sun. Not even the golden rays associated with this magic hour could soften the harshness of the living quarters.

He cautiously navigated the three broken cement steps and the creaking wood slats of the porch and then rang the doorbell. He didn't hear anything, so he pushed it again then followed up

with a rap on the old screen door that held no
screen.

Inside he heard what sounded like either three
dogs bark, or one really big one.

He stepped back from the door and waited.

A tattered curtain moved in the window to his
left. He was debating whether or not to wave
when the door opened up and he was staring at
an older woman wearing a flowered housecoat
and a black hairnet, a cigarette dangling from the
side of her mouth with an ash on it an inch long.
"Whatever you're selling, we ain't buying."

Colin tried to make a physical connection between the woman in front of him and Lucky, but
fell way short of the mark. "Apologies, ma'am,
but I'm not a salesman," he said when she moved
to close the door in his face. "I'm looking for
Miss Clayborn?"

Dark eyes squinted out at him as she removed
the cigarette from her lips, mindless of the ash
that fell to the floor next to the three dogs yapping
at her feet and pawing at the screen door. "What
do you want with Lucky?"

Colin didn't realize he was hoping that he'd
gotten the address wrong until that moment. "I'm
a…friend."

The woman gave him a long once-over then

gave a doubtful grunt. "She lives in the apartment in the back."

The door slammed in his face, leaving Colin standing staring dumbly at the chipped wood.

He made his way back down the stairs and around the side of the house. He could just make out the grille of Lucky's old Chevy parked in the back. His throat grew tight at the knowledge that she was home and he would soon be face-to-face with her. Suddenly it didn't matter that he had to watch where he stepped. Or that this house should have been on somebody's demolition list years ago. All that mattered was that he was going to see Lucky for the first time in a week.

He had to round the house entirely before he finally saw the door to what had to be the back apartment. At one time it had probably been the back door leading to the house's kitchen. The window next to the door was cracked open and he made out the sounds of the same oldies station he listened to and the scent of strawberries. He heard a clang then a soft, "damn."

Colin swallowed hard then lifted his hand to knock.

More sounds from inside, then the door opened, "I told you I'd have the rent..."

Her words stopped as she stared into Colin's

face. A kitchen towel was wrapped around her left hand and she wore a black cotton sundress that seemed to emphasis the deep red of her hair and the paleness of her skin.

"Colin," she breathed more than said.

Realizing he should probably say something, he stuffed his hands inside his pockets to keep from reaching out for her and said, "You didn't make your appointment today."

She blinked at him. "Oh, God. Is it Monday already?"

He looked both ways, feeling awkward standing outside. "May I come in?"

She squinted at him, pulling the towel tighter around her hand. "No."

Colin looked over her shoulder, wondering if someone else was with her. But unless the person had gone to the bathroom, he couldn't see anyone else inside her apartment, a room no larger than his living room. A single mattress was on the floor in one corner, the faded flowery sheets rumpled as if she'd just crawled from it. A small battered table with two mismatched chairs sat beside that, and then there was a sink, a microwave and a two-burner hotplate on the opposite side of the room. In the sink he made out a stainless-steel colander filled with fresh strawberries. Behind the sink sat five or six bottles of alcohol in various states of emptiness.

Lucky caught the direction of his gaze then stepped out next to him and closed the door. "Look, tell Dr. Szymanski I'm sorry I missed my appointment. I worked closing last night at my new job after working the morning shift at my other job and I…" She stared at the blood staining the towel. "And I guess I slept late this morning."

Colin held his hands out. "Let me have a look."

"I didn't think you were that kind of doctor."

His gaze flicked to her smiling face. His relief to see her looking more like herself was complete and startling. "Shut up and give me your hand."

She raised a brow. "Ah, the prominent doctor goes native."

Instead of waiting for her to offer, Colin took her hand gently in his and began unwrapping the towel. He marveled at how small and delicate her fingers were in contrast to his larger ones as he ferreted out the source of the blood. There was a small cut on the outer edge of her index finger, likely made by a knife.

"I was cutting strawberries."

He nodded, thinking about how cool her skin felt against his warmer fingers.

"We should rinse this out with water and bandage it properly."

He didn't miss her shifting her weight back and forth on her bare feet. Feet that were as small and delicate as her hands. And that were attached to the sexiest legs he'd seen in a good long while.

He caught her tugging on the hem of her sundress. A dress that was easily six inches longer than some of the miniskirts he'd seen her in. Why would she be self-conscious about the way she looked now?

She was nervous, he realized. But why? She glanced over her shoulder at the closed door.

"Look, is that all you wanted?" she asked, running her free hand through her tousled red hair.

"No," he said, realizing he'd meant it. "I thought you and I might have a talk."

She narrowed her green eyes at him. Eyes devoid of makeup and doubly intoxicating. "Talk?"

He grinned. "Yes. You know that thing that two people do when they have something to say to each other."

She glanced over her shoulder again.

"Lucky?"

"Hmm? Oh. Okay. I guess it wouldn't hurt to

talk. There's a restaurant down the street there. Meet me there in, say, fifteen?''

She wanted him to meet her somewhere else.

It didn't make sense to Colin. But he wasn't about to argue the point. She'd agreed to talk to him. That should be enough.

Strangely, though, it wasn't.

''Okay. I'll see you in fifteen.''

6

LUCKY CLOSED the door then leaned against it for support, her heart beating a million miles a minute. An upbeat oldies tune filled the small, shabby apartment. She reached for the radio and switched it off then absently wrapped the towel back around her finger.

Colin had come to her apartment.

Colin had seen where she lived.

She rushed to her bed and began straightening the sheets, then she reached for the clothes left on the floor when she'd taken them off early that morning. She started to shove them into the full laundry basket in the corner, then stopped and fished out the white blouse she needed to wear for work again that night.

Next she returned to the fresh strawberries she'd been cleaning in the sink, her movements manic, her mind racing with what he'd seen…and more importantly, what he must have thought of it.

She realized she hadn't cleaned her cut so she unwound the towel then thrust her hand under running water and closed her eyes.

The only person other than herself who had seen where she lived was her landlady, and that was only because she owned the joint. There was something…intimate about being inside someone's place. It left you vulnerable in ways that were hard to explain. And she was very guarded about letting anyone inside her apartment. She'd learned that lesson the hard way when she was seventeen and had rented a room in a downtown flophouse. She'd brought her boyfriend home only to wake up to find everything but the bedsheets she lay on gone. He'd even taken her clothes, which she'd later found out he'd given to his other girlfriend, who had thought he'd bought them.

She'd immediately moved out of the room and into another and had never made the mistake of inviting anyone to where she lived again.

She opened her eyes and her gaze settled on the bottles of liquor sitting on the back of the sink. Had he seen them? She swallowed hard then grabbed the two with only an ounce or two left in them and threw them away. But she hesitated when she reached for the others. The bottles and their contents were sometimes all that stood between her and insanity.

She switched the water off, realizing she should be getting ready to meet Colin. She had little doubt that he'd come back here if she didn't show. He'd come this far already, it likely wouldn't take much to make him return.

The thought motivated her into action.

COLIN GLANCED DOWN at his watch. Twenty-five minutes since he'd agreed to meet Lucky at the restaurant in fifteen. He nudged his watched around his wrist then straightened it. Was she standing him up? Had her agreeing to meet him only been a ruse to get him to leave her place so she could disappear?

He accepted a refill on his coffee and thanked the waitress then sat back in his chair. Tonight he'd seen a different Lucky. She hadn't been the seductress who had thrown herself at him twice at his office. Nor had she been the sassy waitress who had gotten fired from her last job. No, this Lucky…this Lucky had been somehow more exposed. As if he'd caught her off guard and she hadn't been able to recover from the surprise of finding him outside her door.

He sipped at his black coffee without really

tasting it. And she'd been so damn sexy it had taken everything that he had not to sweep her up in his arms and carry her to that mattress on the floor.

Sure, he'd seen places similar to hers. But usually they belonged to college kids who were just scraping by until they graduated. And Lucky was no college kid. She was a full-grown woman who obviously was having a hard time making the rent.

That, he wasn't used to.

"That coffee strong?"

Colin blinked up to find Lucky taking the seat across from him.

At the sight of her, his every muscle relaxed at the same time a simmering heat worked its way under his skin.

She'd put on a pair of snug jeans and a clingy black T-shirt, strappy leather sandals rounding out her casual appearance. She'd applied makeup, but not much. And her hair was pulled back into a neat ponytail, making him want to pull off the rubber band and let the sensual waves fall over her shoulders.

"It's good," he said in response to her question, motioning for the waitress to bring her a cup.

There was a simple black leather tie around her left wrist. For some reason he couldn't quite explain, Colin was fascinated with the piece of jewelry. Perhaps because it seemed to mirror the qualities of its owner. Or perhaps because it brought to mind leather bonds and soft moans.

"You said you wanted to talk?" she asked, adding cream and sugar to her coffee, then using both hands to lift it and take a sip.

He narrowed his gaze. "Morgan nearly reported your absence to the court."

"Nearly. That means she didn't."

He nodded. "I talked her out of it. Promised I'd look into it."

Lucky's shoulders seem to loosen. "Thanks." She smoothed back her already smooth hair. "I really don't need that hassle on top of everything else."

"You're late on your rent?"

She refused to meet his gaze. While she might have forgotten about what she'd said when she'd opened the door and thought he was someone else, he hadn't.

But her stance told him that didn't mean she had any intention of answering his question.

Anyway, what did it matter to him whether or not she could make her rent? Was he prepared to pull his money out and loan her the amount to tide her over until her next paycheck? Was she even working a steady job, or did she move from place to place without ever managing to save a dime?

These were all questions he wanted answers to, but questions he didn't dare ask.

Instead he said, "I guess you don't get very many visitors."

She finally lifted her eyes to him, the expression on her face downright sexy. "You guess correctly."

"Why?"

"Playing therapist again, Dr. McKenna?"

"No. I'm trying to be your friend."

He watched as she shifted uncomfortably. "I don't need any friends."

About to sip his coffee, Colin froze. "Everyone needs friends, Lucky."

"What I meant is that I don't need any more friends."

Why did he get the impression that's not what she meant at all and that her first comment was the more honest one?

Was it possible that the woman across from him didn't have a single friend? Not even one person, forget a whole network of people, she could count on when the clouds obscured the sun and when she needed help in making the rent every now and again?

"Then accept me as your big brother," he said, closely watching her pretty face. "Or don't you need any more family, either?"

Her smile was decidedly provocative. "Why brother? Why not Sugar Daddy?"

"Is that what you want me to be?"

"I don't want you to be anything. You came to see me, remember?"

Oh, yes, he remembered.

He felt something touch his ankle under the table and realized it was her toes. He glanced to find she'd slipped out of her sandal and was working his sock down until her skin touched his. Heat sure and swift swept through his groin.

He cleared his throat.

He got the distinct feeling that she was trying to distract him with sex. And he'd be damned if he was willing to allow her to do it. The truth was he'd been wanting her for so long now that his desire was taking on a life of its own.

"I take it going back to your place is not an option," he said quietly.

She shook her head, keeping her gaze even with his.

He peeled off money to cover the coffee and a generous tip. "Well, then, my place it is."

IF IT WAS TRUE that a place said a lot about the person, then what did Colin's apartment say about him?

Lucky stood just inside the door of the penthouse apartment, taking in the rich leather furniture, the paintings, the brass lamps, and thought that it said that he was wealthy.

"Having second thoughts?" he asked, shrugging out of his suit jacket then loosening his tie as he headed toward what she guessed was his bedroom.

She watched his backside, the tension she'd felt as she followed him to the downtown building reaching a pressure point. She thought about following him but found it impossible to move from the spot where she stood.

"There's some wine in the fridge if you want some."

"How about a beer?"

A pause then, "There may be one or two in there. Why don't you check?"

Lucky craned her neck to look down the hallway where he'd disappeared, then the other way, which she guessed led to the kitchen. She switched on the light inside a cavernous room with terra cotta floor tiles and a woodblock island, thinking it looked better than some of the nicer restaurants she'd worked in.

And it revealed absolutely zero about the man who owned it.

She moved toward the industrial-sized refrigerator. She spotted four or five bottles of imported beer immediately, but as she pulled out two she paused to examine the remainder of the fridge's contents. She smiled at the box of pizza and the half-empty container of chip dip, then opened the freezer to find it well stocked with gourmet-style frozen dinners, vegetables and chocolate-almond ice-cream bars.

She put the beers down on the island, found a plate, then filled it with the leftover pizza, after sniffing it to make sure it was all right. She nuked it, then went back out into the living room at the same time Colin re-entered the room from the other side.

Lucky froze at the sight of him looking like an average guy.

She swallowed hard. Not that she thought him a super stud or anything. But she'd never seen him wear anything but suits, so catching him in jeans and a navy-blue T-shirt and bare feet caught her off guard.

"Hungry?" he asked.

She blinked at the plate of pizza.

He crossed to her, took the plate and the beers from her then carried them to a gaming table against the far wall where he put them down. Lucky followed, running her fingertip along the inlaid wood chessboard that was part of the table and trying not to notice the way the soft denim molded to his backside. Colin pulled a cord and the white curtains opened.

She caught her breath for a second time, staring at another view she'd never seen from this angle before. That of downtown Toledo and the Maumee River at dusk.

"Yeah. That was pretty much my reaction when I saw it. It's the reason I bought the place."

He owned, not rented, the apartment.

But of course he would. Renting was for people like her who lived from hand to mouth.

"Do you want to go outside?" he asked, motioning toward the French doors and the wrought-iron furniture on the balcony beyond.

She shook her head, glanced at her hands, which she was wringing, and found something else to do with them. More specifically, entwine them in Colin's thick, dark blond hair while she kissed him.

ONE MINUTE COLIN had been wondering what to say to Lucky, the next he was kissing her as if it wasn't the pizza he was hungry for but her.

As she launched a breathless attack on his mouth, she pressed her breasts tightly against his chest, her hips bumping his as she sought a closer meeting. He worked his fingers up under the hem of her shirt at the same time she unbuttoned the fly of the jeans he'd just buttoned up. Within seconds she held his rock-hard length in her hands. Colin broke contact with her mouth, groaning aloud. Her touch was gentle yet bold. Her strokes stoked the flames licking through his groin into a full-fledged fire.

Giving up trying to work his own hands under her tight shirt, he instead pulled the stretchy fabric over her head, momentarily pausing their kissing. The instant the fabric was free, her mouth sought his and her hands rested against his throbbing length again.

Never had Colin wanted anyone with the intensity he wanted Lucky. He popped the catch on her bra, then cupped her breasts and greedily licked the swollen mounds of flesh, sucking her right nipple deep into his mouth before switching his attention to her other breast. He heard her low whimper and the sound sent his desire level soaring through the roof.

"I want you so bad I hurt," she whispered, kissing the side of his mouth then moving to his neck.

That was all the incentive Colin needed as he swept her up into his arms.

"No…no," she said, grasping his shoulders tightly. "Not the bedroom."

His steps faltered as he gazed into her passion-filled green eyes.

She smiled. "The couch. I don't think I can wait for the bedroom."

He practically launched her toward his over-stuffed black leather couch where she went to work slipping out of her sandals then shimmying out of her tight jeans. Colin was rooted to the spot, watching as she revealed the skimpiest pair of black underwear he'd ever seen up close and personal. The panties matched her open bra and both matched his couch. She looked as though someone had poured fresh cream over his sofa.

She reached out and yanked him toward her by the pocket of his jeans, reminding him that he had yet to disrobe. He'd begun pulling off his T-shirt when he felt her hot, hot mouth on his straining member.

Dear Lord…

Colin's knees nearly buckled underneath him as he somehow managed to get the shirt off and toss it aside. He stared at Lucky's wild red hair escaping her ponytail and followed the movements of her decadent mouth as she took in as much of his length as she could, then pulled back again. Her hand replaced her mouth and then she went down on him again, nearly draining him as her tongue cradled the sensitive underside of his penis.

As much as he hated to stop her, he wanted their first time to be about mutual sharing. He gently squeezed her shoulders, using every ounce of willpower he had to tug her skillful mouth away from his sensitive flesh. She blinked up at him, obviously confused.

''When I come, I want it to be with you,'' he murmured, kneeling down in front of her.

Something flickered in her eyes, but he couldn't be sure what it was. Surprise? Maybe.

She automatically spread her legs, welcoming him between her slender thighs. He grasped her near the knees then ran his fingers up her supple skin, denting her soft flesh, until his thumbs reached the crotch of her panties. He watched as she sank back into the cushions, giving him full access to her engorged womanhood just beneath the satiny fabric. He lightly stroked the growing wet spot then moved just to the north of it. Her hips bucked involuntarily and he knew he'd hit the target area. Increasing the pressure of his thumb, he started making small circles, listening as her breathing grew more ragged as she tried to fill her lungs with air.

He grabbed the string that made up the side of the panties with his other hand and pulled, satisfied when the material gave, finally baring her to his hungry gaze.

So swollen…so wet…so luscious.

The fabric no longer impeding his progress, he tunneled his thumb through her springy curls and found her fleshy core. Her back came up off the couch and she bore down as if seeking something only he could give her.

He grabbed for his jeans and pulled out the condom he'd put in there not five minutes ago, then quickly sheathed himself, his frantic movements not stopping until he slid into Lucky's sweet flesh to the hilt.

Then everything seemed to stop.

His movements.

His breathing.

His heartbeat.

He met Lucky's gaze, and in the back of his mind he heard what sounded like a low click.

Slowly everything started working again. Double time.

Lucky stared into Colin's dark eyes, mesmerized by the sight of him as he filled her to overflowing. Her heart beat thickly, as if weighed down by a pound of honey. Honey that coated her insides and melted low in her belly, spreading, spreading until she nearly couldn't bear the sheer pleasure it brought.

She sought purchase on the edge of the sofa but found none on the slick leather. So she grasped Colin's shoulders instead, thrusting up to meet him as he withdrew then stroked her again. An agonizing pressure seemed to build up in her very veins and she moaned as his hard arousal slid inside her tight, wet flesh. And, throughout, her gaze was locked with Colin's.

Most men closed their eyes when they had sex. Not Colin. His brown eyes appeared almost black as he watched her watching him. She felt connected to him in a way she hadn't felt connected to anyone before him. Connected by shared pleasure. Ecstasy.

Colin grasped her hips and hauled her down farther so her bottom rested against the edge of the sofa cushion. Then he re-entered her, sending her spiraling ever higher and higher. He withdrew then stroked her again…and again, each thrust faster and deeper than the one before. She felt her breasts sway. Her stomach tremble. Her fingers sink into his shoulders as she rode wave after wave of pure sensation.

Then she felt him stiffen. She bore down on him hard, tilting her hips up then down again, rubbing her pelvis against his.

He groaned, and she joined him in the shared orgasm he'd desired.

7

HOURS LATER Colin lay in his bed next to Lucky, feeling like the luckiest man in the world. He couldn't remember a time when he'd enjoyed sex more. Enjoyed? The word didn't come near to describing his insatiable want of the naked woman curved against him. His fingers still stroked her breast even though she'd fallen into a deep, exhausted sleep a little while before.

He knew if he were to part her swollen flesh and enter her from behind, she'd respond welcomingly. But no matter how much he wanted to do that, to continue what he never wanted to end, he let her rest.

In the dim light filtering in through the floor-to-ceiling windows, her thick hair looked black and her skin seemed to glow eerily white. So beautiful. So responsive. So sensual.

So guarded.

He shifted his hand off her breast and to her flat stomach, pleased by her unconscious shiver.

She was so open to him sexually, yet she'd blocked him from entering her place the night before. What had she been hiding? What hadn't she wanted him to see? It seemed odd that the shameless woman would be ashamed of her own apartment. But what other explanation was there?

He rolled onto his back. Lucky murmured then turned and snuggled up to his side. Colin stared into her sleeping face and finger-combed her hair from her temple. Normally he was the one used to sleeping like the dead after a night of great sex. But somewhere within him he knew that what had happened in the past few hours hadn't just been about sex. It had been great, yes. But it had also been something more.

He squinted at the woman in his arms. She was a sexy enigma to him. So much he didn't know about her. And yet he had invited her into his apartment, his bed, with few reservations, and even those were professional. On a fundamental level he knew he could trust her not to steal the silver. Knew he could count on her not to go through his things while he slept. He wasn't sure how he knew, but he did.

Of course he knew the reason why he couldn't sleep. Beyond his continued and unquenchable want of Lucky was his concern about what would happen in the morning. Would she still be there when he got up? Would she want to share breakfast? Come out and run with him?

He thought of her jeans and sandals and ruled that out. Unless she went back to her place and picked up running gear.

And if she did? Was he ready for things to go so far so fast?

He didn't realize she was watching him until he heard her deep swallow. "You're awake."

The sheets rustled as he covered them both. "So are you."

She flattened her palm against his chest as if wondering at the sight of her skin against his. "What's on your mind?"

He smiled into her hair then kissed her head. "I thought that was my line."

She rubbed her nose against his nipple. "When you're at work it's your line. When you're here…"

Her words seemed to imply she planned to stick around longer than tonight.

She rolled away from him and sat up, her feet over the side of the bed.

Colin resisted the urge to reach for her. "Where are you going?"

"Home."

Home. Back to that ramshackle room on the opposite side of town.

"I was supposed to go in to work tonight."

Colin raised his brows then ran his fingers through his tousled hair. He hadn't even thought to ask what her schedule was. Then again, she hadn't mentioned anything, either.

He watched as she plucked the sheet off her lap and got up. "I guess I have to pound the pavement again in the morning to find another job."

Colin lifted to his elbows, watching as she went into the bathroom. Moments later he heard the sound of the shower. He lay there in the dark, considering what she'd said. He was still there when she emerged from the bathroom smelling like his shampoo and soap then padded out into the living room where he watched her put on her clothes. Moments later she was standing fully dressed in the open doorway.

"Thanks," she said quietly.

"For what?"

"For the great night."

He would have been insulted had he not recognized the humor in her voice.

She began to turn away.

"Lucky?"

She stopped. "What?"

He couldn't make out her beautiful face in the dark. "How much do you need to make your rent?"

She didn't say anything for long moments but he detected a change in her posture. A slight stiffening. "Why? Are you offering to pay it?"

"Yes."

Again, silence.

Then, "No. But thanks for thinking of it."

Colin threw the sheet off and followed her out into the living room. "Then think of it as a loan. You know, until you can get back on your feet."

He caught the flash of her smile. "This is as good as it gets, doc. As much on my feet as I ever am."

He watched as she crossed her arms over her chest.

"Tell me, Colin. Is this where the rich guy feels guilty about banging the poor girl from the wrong side of the tracks and offers to save her from herself?"

Colin felt suddenly, totally exposed standing there in the nude facing her.

"I don't need saving."

She regarded him for a moment, then sighed softly and crossed to stand directly in front of him. She gave him a lingering kiss.

"Thanks, anyway. It was sweet."

He called her a cab, insisting he at least pay for that, then watched as she gathered her purse and let herself out of his apartment.

Colin stood there for long moments, listening as the elevator in the hall dinged open then closed, whooshing Lucky away into the dark night.

Then a thought occurred to him: Maybe it wasn't her he was offering to save.

THE MIDDAY SUN glared against the windshield of Lucky's old Chevy, making the interior of the car almost unbearably hot when it wasn't moving. She adjusted her sunglasses and stared at the red light, wishing it green. The radio issued a burst of static and she reached out to switch it off, leaving nothing but the rumbling sound of the old car vibrating beneath her.

She'd hit no fewer than twenty bars and restaurants in the area and all of them had told her the same thing: they didn't have any openings but if she'd like to fill out an application they'd keep it on file in case something came up.

Lucky blew a long breath out between her lips. She could count the times she'd been contacted that way on one finger. Unless she had an in by knowing someone else who worked at the place or she happened upon a bar where a waiter or waitress had just quit, her chances of landing a position lay somewhere between slim to none. Especially given her spotty work record as of late. While she'd been employed at the pancake house for over a year, her job at Harry's had lasted four months. And her latest gig at the new country-and-western bar and grill near her house had lasted a grand total of six days.

Of course, she wasn't going to tell a prospective boss that the reason for that was she'd chosen sex over a paycheck, so she chose not to mention that job on her applications.

The light finally turned green and she pulled into a strip mall that held several adult dancing clubs. No, she had never danced, and never planned to, but she had worked at one or two as stop gaps until she found something she liked better. The tips were good even if the last time she'd had to wear a string bikini, leather chaps and a cowboy hat when she served the oversexed clientele their expensive drinks.

Dr. Colin McKenna would never be caught dead in a joint like that.

And, she suspected, under normal circumstances neither would he have been caught dead seeing a woman like her.

She pulled into a parking spot facing a strip club and cut the engine. She knew that if she hadn't been assigned to attend counseling at his office the likelihood of their paths crossing would have been low. And even though they had slept together she knew they were about as different as two people could get.

Put simply, she was a twenty-five-year-old Chevy, and he was a brand-spanking new Lincoln Navigator. And while her old muscle car could give his a run for its money any day of the week, at the end of that day it was still an old Chevy.

And she was still the same old Lucky.

Still, the possibility of never seeing him again sent a knife-sharp pain shooting through her chest.

Five minutes later she was still sitting in the car staring at the doors to the strip joint, her hands clenched against the hot steering wheel, her mind firmly on Colin McKenna, when sunlight reflected off a nearby door, snagging her attnetion. Lucky squinted at a customer exiting a shop two doors up from the strip club. A brunette about her age propped open the door then began sweeping the sidewalk. She took in the sign above the store.

Women Only.

Lucky cracked a grin, finding the name apropos

given its location. What else would you name a shop next to a gentlemen's only club?

A Help Wanted sign caught her attention.

She hadn't worked in retail much. She'd found the hours weren't as flexible and the pay without tips not nearly as much as she made as a waitress.

She got out of the car and headed for the strip joint.

Halfway there she switched courses and turned toward the other shop.

The woman cleaning the sidewalk stopped sweeping and looked up at her. Lucky pushed her sunglasses to the top of her head and asked, ''You looking to hire somebody?''

Tsk, tsk. Bad Dr. McKenna.

COLIN STARED at the note he'd found under his windshield wiper outside his apartment building this morning. He didn't have to wonder who had left it. Obviously Jamie was still avidly stalking him.

He resisted the urge to crumple the paper and instead tucked it into the band under his sun visor so he could hand it over to his attorney in his ever-hopeful bid to press stalking charges against his former patient. As he waited for the light to change, he gripped and released the steering wheel.

Obviously last night Jamie had spotted him going back to his place with Lucky. And obviously Jamie thought Lucky might still be one of his patients.

At any rate, he couldn't afford to make any more mistakes like that, as his attorney kept reminding him. "Play it low-key, Colin. We'll just have to hope that Jamie will back off, move on to someone else, and this will all be over with."

Only Jamie wasn't backing off. And he was getting tired of living his life constantly looking over his shoulder.

The traffic in front of him moved forward and he followed suit, turning off into a parking lot a half mile up the road. Will had asked him to meet him for lunch at a rib joint and while he'd rather follow up on what was happening with Lucky, he'd decided a few ribs and some straight talk might be just what the doctor ordered.

Twenty minutes later, well into his second rib, he said to Will, point-blank, "I slept with her last night."

His British friend gave him one of his best poker-faced stares. "Slept with whom?"

Colin put the rib down and wiped his hands on a napkin.

"So," Will said, apparently realizing Colin wasn't going to rise to the bait, "was it everything you imagined it would be?"

Colin met his friend's gaze head-on. "And more."

Will forgot nonchalance and raised his brows. "I was expecting a 'no.'"

Colin grinned. "I know you were. But sorry, mate, I can't give it to you," he said, mimicking his friend's accent.

They ate in silence for a few moments. "That good, huh?" Will asked.

"Mmm. And better."

One night, right after Amanda had left Colin, the two men had finished off a twelve pack of beer and discussed how women might find these male exchanges. Will had surmised that since women romanticized everything, they'd be horrified to hear themselves being referred to by a rating system. Colin had liked to think women were more open-minded than that and had even been privy to a few female conversations where size had definitely been mentioned.

Will finished off his ribs then washed them

down with the rest of his pint of beer. "So when do you take her home to meet the parents?"

Colin's light mood took a dark nosedive.

"Uh-oh. I don't know if I like the looks of that expression."

"You can be such an arrogant ass, do you know that, Will?"

His friend crossed his arms on top of the table. "I daresay my irreverence is one of the things you love about me."

Which was true.

Except his jibe this time had definitely hit the wrong chord.

"So you're not taking her home to meet the parents, then?"

Colin gave up on the rest of his ribs. "We slept together, I didn't propose to her."

"Well, that's good then."

Colin stared at the bubbles lining the walls of his glass of club soda.

"It is good, isn't it?"

"I don't even know if I'm going to see her again."

"Why not? Obviously you enjoyed the sex." Will leaned back and allowed their server to take his plate. Colin bristled at the open way his friend eyed the pretty young waitress, because it made him wonder how often Lucky got the same attention. "Don't tell me. She's making serious noises already." He sighed. "And why not? A doctor like yourself should be a good catch for someone of her station."

He tamped down his irritation at Will's continued underhanded jabs at Lucky. "To the contrary, she didn't indicate one way or another that she wanted to see me again, either."

"But she enjoyed the sex."

"She very definitely enjoyed the sex."

"So what's the problem, mate? By all means have more of it, then."

The problem was that he feared he was hearing his own brand of serious noises in his head.

"So, tell me," he said, deciding he needed to change the subject, "how did everything go with pink ribbon number thirty-two?"

Will gave an exaggerated sigh. "I haven't been half as lucky as you in that department, unfortunately. Get it? Lucky?"

Colin chuckled quietly and listened as his friend told him about his trials and tribulations with a woman who had decided she wasn't going to have sex again until the day she was married.

8

AT TEN O'CLOCK that evening Colin sat on the same sofa he and Lucky had had sex on the night before, a psychology magazine open on his lap, the large-screen television flashing muted pictures of a newsmagazine show.

But his mind was on none of it. Instead his hand absently caressed the rich leather against which Lucky and her flawless skin had lain. And his mind focused on all that she'd said, all that she'd done up until she'd kissed him goodbye and left.

While Will's words at lunch had made him a little hot under the collar, the fact remained that there were some real issues surrounding his connection to Lucky Clayborn.

But none of them stopped him from wanting her with a physical intensity that was foreign to him.

He'd called her number earlier, only to find it was out of service. A casualty of her unstable lifestyle? More than likely. Although he guessed Lucky was the type of person who would change her number just to keep people guessing. Just as she had prevented him from entering her place the night before, so she barred everyone from learning too much about her.

And for that reason he'd restrained himself from stopping by her place again. If he were to be truthful, he was half afraid he'd find she'd already moved on. Or might if he continued to invade her private sanctum.

He wondered how much those bottles behind the sink had to do with finding her peace of mind.

Colin picked up the remote, surfed through a few satellite channels, then he switched off the television altogether. He was all too familiar with addictive personality disorders. And while it was on record that Lucky had claimed her second D.U.I. offense had been the result of cold medication, he couldn't help wondering how often she turned to those myriad bottles at her apartment to help chase away the monsters that were known to come out at night. He glanced toward the chess table set up to his left, recalling that they'd never gotten around to drinking those beers she'd brought them from the kitchen along with the pizza the night before. Also, he'd never detected a hint of liquor on her breath. But that didn't necessarily mean she didn't go back to her place at night and drink herself into a stupor.

He rubbed his face and sighed deeply, pondering what it was about this one woman that fascinated him so. She was prickly to a painful extent, yet soft and sexy and vulnerable. She needed help yet refused it. And she could take him to soaring heights of ecstasy with one little flick of her tongue or tilt of her lush hips.

The downstairs bell rang. He glanced at his watch, then put the magazine down on the coffee table and stepped toward the intercom. "Yes?"

"Colin? It's Lucky. Hope you like chicken balls."

He stood for a long moment grinning, then pressed the button that would allow her access to the lobby and the elevator.

He opened the door and leaned against the jamb. He was still standing there waiting when the elevator finally dinged and the doors opened to reveal her holding up take-out cartons.

"Ah, you were talking about Chinese food," he said dryly.

She snorted inelegantly and brushed past him into his apartment.

Colin briefly closed his eyes, enjoying the scent

of her as she passed. He hadn't truly known how much he was looking forward to seeing her until that moment. Though he'd been darkly contemplating his connection to her only a short time before, now he wore a grin that didn't seem to want to budge. And rather than dreading the rest of the evening he was now looking forward to it.

He turned to find her standing in the middle of the room.

"Where do you want it?" she asked.

Colin considered the provocative way she stood, her legs spaced slightly apart, her weight on one foot, calling attention to the shortness of her skirt and the tightness of her shirt.

"Hmm…I think the bedroom would work."

TWO HOURS LATER Lucky straddled a sitting Colin in the middle of his gigantic bed. She was hot and sticky and she couldn't seem to draw a full breath to save her life as he fondled her breasts, her womb still contracting from her latest climax.

She propped her elbows on his shoulders and entangled her fingers in his hair. "What you do to me," she murmured as she placed open-mouthed kisses all over his face then lingered on his delectable lips.

''What *do* I do to you?'' he asked, nipping at the skin over her collarbone.

She managed to consider his question even as she reveled in the feel of him still filling her, the ache of her muscles from their second night of fantastic sex, and the hot proof of her passion for him wetting her thighs.

''You make me feel like I don't know myself anymore. Like my body doesn't belong to me.''

He chuckled softly and brushed her damp hair back from her face. ''I think that's the first time you've answered a question without challenging it.''

She searched his dark eyes, realizing he was right.

She rolled off him and groaned when her muscles pulled in protest. ''I don't know how much of this I can stand.''

Colin stretched out next to her, idly plucking her closest nipple. ''I can't remember having so much fun in the sack.''

She smiled as she stroked the hand that stroked her. ''Then you've been missing out, doc.''

The bedding rustled as he shifted next to her. ''No, it's not that, Lucky. It's…''

His words trailed off, causing her heartbeat to thicken.

"I don't know about you, but that Chinese is looking awfully good to me right now."

She climbed from the bed, put on her panties and her tank, then padded into the other room where she'd left the food cartons. The dim apartment's only was illumination was golden pools of light from the moon that loomed large outside the windows. She wasn't surprised when she felt Colin's mouth against her shoulder and his ever-present arousal against her bottom.

"Here," she said, handing him a carton over her shoulder along with chopsticks. "I hope you like Kung Pao chicken."

"Mmm." He seemed to like her flesh even more as he continued to nibble and lick. "I'd die for some Kung Pao chicken."

He finally took the carton and they sat down across from each other at the gaming table against the window. As Lucky opened a carton of shrimp-fried rice and took a bite, she considered the view that lay ten floors below. The lights from the High Level Bridge twinkled, though she suspected it was more a trick of the wind. The waters of the Maumee River glistened darkly, sailboats anchored on this side of it, large ocean-going tankers on the opposite side. Spotlighted flags flapped lazily in the light breeze at International Park across the way, and it seemed every other window was still lit in the thirty-floor Owens-Illinois Building to the right of the Cherry Street Bridge.

She'd never really seen the city she'd grown up in from this vantage point. Shadows and cracked asphalt and roaring traffic was more a part of the vista outside her apartment window. But at least there were crickets and lightning bugs. Here she suspected there would be none.

"So what happened with your job?"

She blinked Colin's handsome face into view. The pale light from the moon gave it a bluish cast, making him look even more striking, with his hair sloping over his brow, twelve o'clock shadow darkening his jaw.

She took another bite of rice then shrugged. "They fired me."

His silence spoke volumes.

It seemed she'd taken great pleasure in shocking people for so much of her life that she was having a hard time with talking straight.

"But that's all right. I landed a day job this afternoon."

She wasn't sure why she'd offered up the information. Normally she would have left her end of the conversation at "they fired me." After all, it was nobody's business but her own where she worked, how she survived. And it had been so long since someone had actually worried about her that it was…strange that Colin was now.

"Another bar?"

She smiled. "Do you want something to drink?"

She made her way to the kitchen, then came back with a couple of cans of sodas. She took note of his raised brow as she handed him one.

"What?"

He popped the top of his can and took a sip. "I don't know. I guess I was expecting beer."

She sat back down and picked up her rice again. "No beer tonight. I want to be fresh when I start tomorrow morning at Women Only."

"Sounds like a strip joint."

She laughed quietly. "It's a…actually, I'm not really sure what it is. But it's definitely not a strip joint."

She thought about how close she'd come to by-passing the small business and actually going to a strip joint and sighed.

"The pay's not much, but the girl who manages the place…I don't know. I liked her."

"That's good."

Lucky looked across the small table to find Colin staring at her in a way that made the tiny hairs on her arms stand on end. "What?"

His grin made her stomach tremble. "Nothing. I was just thinking about how beautiful you are."

Lucky returned her attention to her rice. She'd never been called beautiful before. Pretty, maybe once or twice. Sexy, definitely. But never beautiful.

But when Colin said it, she almost felt beautiful.

She reached across the table for the package of egg rolls, startled when he grasped her wrist.

"I think it's time for dessert," he whispered.

Before she knew it, she was being tugged into his lap back first.

Lucky gasped as she felt his rock-hard arousal press against her aching womanhood.

"Has anyone ever told you you're insatiable?" she asked thickly.

His hands sought and found her breasts, then dove under the hem of her tank and cupped them tightly. "Has anyone ever told you you're irresistible?"

He shifted them and the chair so that they were facing the window and the vista outside. She shuddered as one of his hands made a beeline for her crotch and stroked her through the material of her panties. Then the hand disappeared from her breast and a floor lamp flicked on next to them. She inhaled sharply when she discovered that the scene outside the window disappeared, the dark glass instead throwing back at her the image of herself straddling Colin. She hadn't realized he hadn't put anything on until that moment. His dark-hair-covered legs were spread, his manhood magnificently displayed beneath her own spread thighs. One of his hands tunneled inside her tank top and cupped her breast and the other worked its way inside her panties, boldly stroking her.

The sight was so powerfully erotic Lucky shuddered from head to foot. She found his hands with hers, covering them as he caressed and fondled her, until it was not only his hands doing the stroking, but her own as well.

An unbearable pressure built up low, low in her abdomen as he bit into her shoulder then pushed aside the crotch of her panties to reveal the dark-auburn thatch of hair there. He parted her damp flesh, showing her the core of her womanhood as his rigid shaft slid against it.

Lucky moved her hands to his knees and arched her back, her movements placing the knob of his arousal against her slick portal. A simple shift of her hips and he would breach the barrier. But rather than reaching for the condoms she noticed he'd put on the table, she worked her flesh down the length of him and back, avoiding penetration, reveling in the feel of her juices sluicing over his turgid flesh.

His left hand disappeared from between her legs and he was reaching around her to sheath himself. Then, finally, he thrust deep inside her. Lucky instantly climaxed, shuddering all around him as she clutched his legs for balance. He stayed still, his gaze connected to hers in the glass. As soon as her spasms abated, he began to thrust again, his length entering and withdrawing.

A low, primal moan escaped from Lucky's throat as she tilted her hips to meet his hungry lunges. His hands tightly gripped her waist, bringing her down harder and faster, making it impossible for her to catch her breath. In the glass her breasts bounced, her hair tumbled, and her mouth bowed open as flesh slapped against flesh, hard disappeared into soft, and she tumbled into a land she had never dared imagine existed.

She watched as Colin threw his head back and clenched his teeth, on the brink of orgasm. The moment his body stiffened, she bore tightly down against him and ground her hips, hitting spots that guaranteed she would chase right after him with a second climax.

For long minutes afterward, neither of them moved but for their ragged breathing. Then Colin was touching her again, his fingers branding her breast and her clit.

"I love to touch you," he whispered harshly, kissing and licking her shoulder.

"I love it when you touch me."

He grasped her hips and slowly withdrew, then tugged her so she straddled him from the front, putting them face-to-face. Lucky could no longer see their reflection in the glass. But she knew he could. She made the maneuvers necessary to strip herself of her shirt and panties, exchange Colin's condom for a fresh one, then climb back on top of him. She tossed her hair so that it fell in long waves down the middle of her bare back, then pushed out her bottom so that all was revealed in the glass behind her.

She heard Colin's deep groan then felt his fingers on her bottom where he parted her even further from behind so he could get a better look. She positioned herself directly over his rigid shaft then sank slowly down, well aware of the show she was providing for him. She was determined to create an experience he would never forget…and in turn earn herself an orgasm that she would always remember.

9

THREE DAYS LATER the manager of Women Only said to Lucky, "You have the look of a woman well sexed."

Renae Truesdale was a few inches shorter than Lucky, but that didn't detract from her dynamic presence. Around the same age as Lucky, Renae seemed to vibrate with a vivid vitality and sexuality most women would envy. Lucky had taken an immediate liking to her that first day when she'd approached her on the sidewalk. And three days later she felt the same.

Renae twisted her lips. "If we could bottle what put that look on your face, we'd be very rich women."

Normally Lucky might have offered up a sarcastic comeback. Maybe something along the lines of "who needs rich when there's great sex to be had?"

Now she merely smiled. Though her mind provided the jibe, something held her back from making light of what was happening between her and Colin. She didn't dare delve into what exactly that something was. She'd learned long ago that today, the moment, was all that mattered. What sense was there in looking down the road when that same road might narrow into a dark and cruel dead end?

Renae began to help Lucky fold the thick, Turkish terry-cloth robes that had come in that morning and put them on the display shelves against the far wall of the shop. From bath and lingerie stuffs to massage oils and aromatherapy candles, Women Only was packed full of everything a woman could want, and many things only a woman could understand. Lucky had yet to see one man come through the door. Not that she could blame the opposite sex. They'd probably feel as lost as she would at a sports supply store.

One of the many fringe benefits of her new job was that yesterday Renae had packed a boxful of things for her to use at home. As she'd put it, "You can't recommend a product unless you've used and liked it."

In Lucky's case, Colin had enjoyed the products as much, if not more, than she had last night.

"You're doing a good job, Lucky," Renae said, leaning into her in a way that might have made Lucky a little wary a short time ago but that she found herself welcoming now. "I'm impressed with your work so far. Even a couple of customers have commented on how much they like you."

Lucky had never really received compliments on her work and she hadn't expected to. Generally she was only spoken to when a table needed waiting, drinks needed serving and when she wasn't keeping up with the hectic pace.

She didn't know quite how to respond. "I like it here," she said, and found that was the truth.

To her, a job had always been a job, judged by the tips she brought home rather than how she passed the time. She'd chosen the places where she'd worked by how busy they'd keep her, because when she was busy she didn't have time to think. It was hard to think about the landlady wanting the rent or the phone company threatening to shut off your line when you were occupied with serving food before it got cold or refilling a customer's drink.

The front-door bell rang and a woman came in, issued a brief greeting to Renae, then headed straight for the back where a room decorated in white with red candles was separated from the rest of the shop.

Renae put the last robe on the pile in front of her. "Time for my eleven o'clock."

Lucky knew that was her cue to hold down the shop. Renae waited a moment to give the woman time to change into a robe and stretch out on the massage table, then she joined her, striking up a conversation as she pulled the thick, red velvet curtain closed behind her, blocking the two from view.

A massage sounded really good right now. Sex with Colin was introducing her to all sorts of muscles she hadn't known she had.

The bell on the door rang again. Lucky gathered the empty box, stashed it behind the counter then turned toward the customer. "May I help you?" she asked.

A pretty blonde wearing a trendy red sleeveless mock turtleneck and white pants smiled at her.

"You must be Lucky. Hi, I'm Leah Bur—um, West." She laughed. "Sorry, I'm not quite used to my married name yet."

Leah. Now that rang a bell. She realized it was because Leah was the owner of the Women Only satellite shop on the opposite end of town. A place she'd heard described as putting the *P* in posh that was already garnering a lot of attention in the local media.

"Nice to meet you. You're right, I'm Lucky. But not enough to win the lottery," she said with a wry smile at her lame joke.

Leah laughed and Lucky took the unguarded moment to examine the other woman's features. Renae was right. You could tell when a woman was well sexed.

Huh.

"I called Renae to tell her I'd be stopping by to stock up on a few supplies until I receive replacement shipments." She picked up a jasmine-scented candle, put it down, then lifted a vanilla one. "I shouldn't be long so don't worry about having to entertain me."

Lucky smiled. "Okay. Just wave if you need anything."

She went to work on collapsing the empty box, dusting the glass display case and marking down some of the items of inventory they might need to replenish soon.

The bell rang again. She turned to find Colin standing inside the door looking about as comfortable as a pup in a lion's den. A very handsome and sexy pup.

Lucky's heart skipped a beat. She'd never had anyone visit her on the job before.

Colin's gaze moved to her and she smiled widely at him. He seemed to relax instantly.

"Yes, sir, is there something I can do to help you?" she said in a tone teasing enough for him to understand she was glad to see him, yet benign enough in case Renae was listening.

Leah West had spotted the new visitor. "Dr. McKenna? Colin, is that you?"

COLIN WAS HELPLESS to explain what happened to him every time his sight was filled with Lucky's beautiful face. His breathing seemed to grow shallower, his libido leapt to attention, and his chest tightened in an unfamiliar way. He recognized that the symptoms weren't a simple matter of sex. While he knew indescribable pleasure when their limbs were intertwined, his want of her was beginning to surpass that surface, physical need. He wanted to be with her, hear her laugh, listen to her opinion on issues that mattered to her, and just plain look at her.

"It is you! Imagine that."

Colin finally glanced at the woman who had said his name. He smiled. "Leah. It's good to see you."

She extended her hand and he shook it, noticing that there was something different about the woman he had counseled along with her ex-husband a couple of short months ago.

"I received your wedding invitation. I'm sorry I couldn't make it."

Leah's brown eyes sparkled. "I take it you noticed the name of the husband had changed."

He nodded. "I not only noticed, I expected it, Leah. And I'm happy for you."

He remembered Leah and her ex-husband, Dan Burger, well, if only because they had been the only couple he'd counseled recently who'd stood a chance of true reconciliation. Not because they'd been a love match. That much had been obvious even to him. But because for whatever reasons each of them held, they'd wanted it to work.

Still, he was secretly glad it hadn't. Settling was no way to go into a union that was supposed to last a lifetime.

On that thought his gaze drifted to Lucky. She was watching the exchange with interest, but made it clear she didn't want to interfere.

"Leah, have you met Lucky?" he said.

LUCKY WASN'T SURE what surprised her more, that Colin was introducing her to Leah, or that she was happy that he was.

"Yes, we've met," Lucky said. "Mrs. West happens to own the sister shop of Women Only."

She watched as Colin's brow rose and he congratulated the other woman on her recent accomplishments, indicating she'd undergone quite a change since he'd last seen her and that the changes suited her.

Lucky covertly watched Colin. Aside from her first group session at his office, she hadn't observed him much around other people. She decided she liked what she saw. A lot. He exuded a commanding presence, and not only because of his size. There was something about him that made you feel welcome and safe and happy all at once. Or at least that's how he made her feel.

Leah looked at her. "I think I have everything I need for now." She held out a slip of paper and Lucky took it. "This is a list of the items I took. Tell Renae I'll replace them by the end of the week at the latest."

Lucky nodded, they exchanged pleasantries, and then the doorbell clanged as Leah left.

Suddenly she and Colin were completely, totally, utterly alone.

Well, except for Renae and her client in the back.

Colin cleared his throat. The telltale sign of nervousness made Lucky smile.

"Nice place," he said.

Lucky looked around. "Yes, it is, isn't it?"

"I came by to see if you have time to catch a bite with me. I'm on my way downtown for a couple of meetings and had a little free time on my hands."

The way his gaze raked over her face and body, she had the feeling that he'd like to have his hands full of much more than free time.

Lucky shivered. "Sorry, my lunch break isn't until two."

He nodded, then shook his head. "Shame."

She agreed. "Damn shame."

"Okay, then, I'll see you later?" he asked.

She nodded.

He began walking toward the door, then hesitated. Taking something out of his pocket, he came back to stand in front of her. He grasped her hand and placed something in the middle of her palm. "I may run a little a late. Why don't you let yourself in?"

Lucky stared down at the key resting against her skin. But she didn't have a chance to respond as he kissed her then left her standing in the middle of the room to make of the exchange what she would.

ONCE A MONTH for the past three years Colin had sat in on group sessions at a local shelter for teenage runaways. His original commitment with Crossroads had been for a year, but when the period had been up, he'd found he couldn't turn away from the nonprofit agency or its boarders. While the stories of abuse and neglect often made him feel sick to his stomach, the resiliency and determination of the teens never failed to awe and inspire him.

This month, as every month, there were at least five new additions to the group, and he noticed that three others were missing, likely having moved back home, in with relatives, or having been placed with foster families. In some sad cases, a few emotionally damaged teens exchanged life at the home for life on the streets.

There were a few mandatory requirements that the boarders met, and one of them was attending these sessions. Considering the members, Colin always left his jacket and tie in his car and folded up the sleeves and unbuttoned the collar of his shirt. Today's session was beginning to wind down.

As he listened to a thirteen-year-old named Melissa talk of her absent, uncaring father and her physically abusive stepmother, who had thrown out all the sentimental items that meant something to the girl, Colin found his mind drifting to Lucky.

A shadow skittered around on the outer edges of his thoughts but he couldn't quite hold on to it long enough to get a better look.

Melissa finished and the housemother cleared her throat, then called the session to an end.

Colin looked down at the notes he'd written. He generally stayed over in case any of the teens wanted to talk to him one-on-one with the housemother present, and also to consult with the housemother on others' progress. The group sessions were designed to allow the teens to air their problems, work through them, and understand that they weren't alone, that there were not only others like them, there were others who had it worse.

That realization alone was often enough to help the teens move beyond the past and begin working toward a better future. A future they were in control of.

Again that sensation of missing something haunted him.

"Dr. McKenna, can I talk to you for a minute?"

He blinked up at Melissa, the last teen to speak, and smiled. Some of the others left to see to house chores, go to jobs outside the home, but most of them lingered on, gathering into smaller groups and continuing the rap session on a smaller scale.

Colin patted the spot next to him on the couch he sat on in the room set up to be comfortable rather than utilitarian. There were no hardback chairs here. Only cozy armchairs and sofas arranged in a circle.

''What's on your mind, Melissa?'' he asked, determined to fully dedicate the next few minutes to the thirteen-year-old with the eyes of a thirty-year-old.

LATER THAT NIGHT Colin returned to his place, not realizing how much he'd been looking forward to seeing Lucky until he opened the door to a dark apartment. He flicked on a light and glanced around, but found no sign that Lucky was either there or had been there. He tossed his keys to the hall table then looked at his watch. Just after nine.

Over the past few days they had settled into a routine of sorts. Lucky knocked off at the shop at around six and by six-thirty she was at his place. They usually ordered in food and spent the night indulging in all sorts of wicked pleasures. That's why it had seemed natural for him to give her his key earlier.

Why, then, wasn't she there?

He absently rubbed the back of his neck and checked his home voice mail. A message from his car insurance company following up a small claim he'd made recently, a hello from his mother who just wanted to catch up with him and then... nothing.

A brief knock sounded on the door behind him. He glanced toward it then moved to open it.

Lucky stood in the hall holding up his key. ''I think this belongs to you.''

He hesitantly accepted the key back, noticing the wary expression on her face. She came inside and he closed the door after her.

It struck him that if given the same type of access to his place, another woman would have put an extra toothbrush next to his. Put a change of clothes and underwear in his drawers. Somehow stamped her presence subtly but meaningfully all over the place, much as a cat marked its territory.

But not Lucky.

Of course he'd already known that she wasn't like most women. It was just taking him a while to figure out how unlike them she was.

"I placed an order for a large pizza before I came over so it should be here any minute," she said, putting her purse on the hall table and walking toward the kitchen, much as she had the past few nights. "Soda?"

No mention of why she had knocked on the door instead of letting herself in with the key. No reference to why she happened to show up at the same time he had instead of letting herself in earlier.

He watched as her shapely bottom disappeared into the kitchen, and then her delectable front faced him as she handed him a can of soda.

"There's a new show on Fox. Do you mind if we catch a little of it?"

Colin shook his head.

But before she could completely turn away from him, he said quietly, "Lucky, we need to talk."

10

IF THERE WERE any four words in the English language Lucky hated, it was those four.

"We need to talk."

Usually when she heard them it meant she was about to be fired or let go or laid off.

Only Colin wasn't her boss.

Still, the graveness of his tone told her she probably wasn't going to like what he had to say.

"About what?" she asked, trying to play it off while knowing her chances of getting away with it with the sexy doc lay between slim and none.

He held up the key in his hand.

Lucky looked from it to him. "What about it?"

"Why didn't you use it?"

She popped the tab on her soda and took a long swallow, somehow managing to get the liquid past her tight throat. "There was no need to. You were already home."

His eyes narrowed. "Convenient."

She smiled and turned toward the couch. "Wasn't it though?"

She found the remote tucked in between the seat cushions and switched on the large-screen television that was probably worth more than she brought home in a month. She found the station she was looking for then crossed her legs in front of her, her short shorts short but enough to cover her decently.

Depending on your definition of decent.

Colin sat down next to her. Peripherally she watched as he put the extra house key down on the coffee table in front of them and fought not to stare at her shorts.

He quietly cleared his throat. "Did you stay past closing time at the shop?"

"Hmm?" she asked, pretending an interest in the show that had just started.

He gestured with his hand. "Work. Did you work overtime today?"

"No."

They sat like that for long minutes, neither of them saying anything, Lucky feeling his gaze on her profile while she stared at the television.

Then he picked up the remote and switched off the show.

"Hey, I was watching that," she said.

The expression on his face was far too serious. She decided it needed to be kissed off.

"Looks like somebody had a rough day," she murmured. Climbing to her knees, she wrapped her arms around his neck, placed her forehead against his, then leisurely pressed her lips against his. When he didn't immediately respond, she ran her tongue along the length of his bottom lip, then slowly slipped it inside his mouth, teasing him, tempting his tongue to come out and play.

He groaned, his hand finding the back of her neck and pulling her forward as he gave in to her attentions and kissed her back. In no time at all, they were both going at it hot and heavy, Lucky grateful for the surge of sensual need snaking through her.

Then Colin's grip increased on the back of her neck and he hauled his mouth from hers, his breath hot on her cheek. "Distracting me with sex, no matter how tempting, is not going to work this time, Lucky."

She pulled slightly back and stared deep into his eyes.

"Why didn't you use the key?"

Desire still throbbed with a life of its own through her body, even though his words served as a bucket of cold water over her intentions.

She reluctantly sat back across the sofa from him. "Because this isn't my place."

"No, it's mine. And I gave you a key so you could come over early."

Too soon, an inner voice said.

Only that wasn't true, either, was it? Unless her subconscious was alerting her that it was too soon to end her relationship with Colin.

Her heart gave such a hard squeeze she nearly gasped.

"Don't treat me like a child, Colin."

"I'm not treating you like a child. I'm a man who would like to have an issue addressed and I'm calmly asking you to address it. Why didn't you use the key?"

She stared at him, realizing he wasn't going to give up until he got an answer.

So she gave him the only one she had.

"I didn't want to use the damn key, that's why. Is that enough for you?"

She shifted uncomfortably on the sofa, curving one of her legs under herself.

"And the reasoning behind that...?"

"Because I didn't feel comfortable coming in here when you weren't home, Colin. Isn't that enough?"

"Why? What could you do while I wasn't here that you couldn't while I am?"

She made a scoffing sound. "You'd be surprised."

He didn't say anything for a few moments, then asked, "What are you saying? That you might be tempted into doing something I wouldn't like if I left you here by yourself?"

"Now you're putting words into my mouth."

Frustration bracketed his sexy mouth. "Well, somebody has to, because you're not offering any up."

Lucky looked at him long and hard. Colin McKenna touched her in ways she couldn't begin to describe. Along with being the sexiest guy she'd ever met, he didn't pass judgment on her because of their differences. He was generous to a fault.

And he'd given her the key to his place—even if it was for a single use—mere days after they'd first slept together.

But she could do without the third degree. She liked having to worry only about herself. And she didn't particularly like when others started butting into her business.

She fidgeted, feeling more than a little agitated. "What is it with shrinks and their habit of talking everything to death?"

He didn't even blink in the face of the criticism. "What is it with beautiful stubborn women afraid to share how they're feeling?"

She held his straight gaze for a long moment, and then a smile began working its way up from her heart to her mouth. "Touché. I guess I deserved that one."

His return grin eased her ruffled feathers. "While I, on the other hand, didn't deserve the shrink jibe." He put his hand on her knee.

The movement was so natural, so unaffected, that her stomach pitched to somewhere in the vicinity of her feet.

It made her want to coax the skillful limb a little farther to the north. If only to chase away the unwanted thoughts clouding her mind and help her focus on something else.

She briefly closed her eyes. "What if I told you I didn't use your key today because…because it…this…is moving too fast for me?"

The fingers on her knee tightened.

He didn't answer so she cracked open her eyes, half expecting him to call her a liar.

Instead, he nodded, appearing unhappy with the question but open to it. "Then I'd have to accept that's how you feel."

Lucky maneuvered herself on the sofa until she

was curved against his side. Both of them stared at the opposite wall, their fingers intertwined on her knee.

She wasn't sure how he knew, but she was fully aware that he realized her answer wasn't the true reason why she hadn't used his key earlier, why she had waited until now to come over so she wouldn't have to use it.

But she was grateful that he didn't pursue the matter.

Maybe it was because he sensed that to pursue it would be to end it.

"You know," he said quietly, rubbing his temple against her hair, "I've been looking forward to this moment all this day. This time when I could see you again...touch you."

Lucky took a deep breath and smiled into the side of his neck.

"Me, too," she admitted, surprised by how easily the admission came...and how outside the norm it was for her.

And how very much she wanted to have this man inside her again, stroking her until the outside world no longer existed.

She got up and held her hand out to him.

He hesitated, then put his into it, allowing her

to lead him to the bedroom, the imminent pizza delivery, and the key momentarily forgotten.

Momentarily…

COLIN AWOKE to the smell of bacon frying.

Sure he was imagining things, he rolled over and groaned into his pillow, only then realizing something was missing from the bed.

Lucky.

He reached for the alarm clock that sat face down on his nightstand and squinted at the time. Just after nine.

Just after nine?

He pushed up to his elbow then ran his hand over his hair and face several times. He couldn't remember the last time he'd slept past seven, even on a Saturday morning. By now he would have been out for his morning run, had his breakfast, read the *Toledo Blade* and *The Wall Street Journal,* and would have been on his way to whatever he had on tap for this morning.

Which happened to be tennis with Will.

He reached for the cordless receiver on the bed-side table and pressed the speed dial for his friend.

''You're late,'' Will said without preamble.

Colin grinned as he swung his feet over the side of the bed. ''Actually, I'm not late yet.''

"'Yet' being code for you're not on your way here, I take it?"

"Mmm. Let me call you back in a half hour."

"Well, what in the hell does that mean?"

"It means what it means."

"Well, holy hell, Colin, how long do you expect me to wait?"

He sensed he was no longer alone and looked toward the door to find Lucky standing in it wearing nothing but the barbecue apron his ex-fiancée had bought for him as a housewarming gift. It said, Master Of All Things Hot.

Colin suddenly had a hard time getting his thoughts together as he followed the white shoulder straps to where they just covered Lucky's bare breasts. Her fiery red hair was slightly damp and framed her face in a riot of sexy curls.

She held a large metal spatula in her right hand and seemed to indicate, if the need arose, she could use it for something other than turning food.

"Will, I'll, um, call you back."

"Jesus, Colin, don't you dare hang up—"

Colin hung up on him then replaced the receiver on the night table.

"Will, as in Dr. Will, your obnoxious friend with the British accent from Harry's?"

Colin's throat tightened as she leaned against

the doorjamb, causing one of the straps to move slightly right of center allowing her nipple to peek out. "That would, um, be him." He stared intently into her face. "Come here."

Her green eyes twinkled at him naughtily. "I would but I'm afraid I might burn something."

"Baby, the only thing burning is me sitting here looking at you looking like that."

She laughed, the throaty sound filling the room, the apartment and Colin's heart with the sweet sound. "Cheesy. Definitely cheesy."

"What matters is the end result."

She seemed to consider his words, slapping the spatula into her opposite palm, her gaze traveling leisurely over his nude body where he sat on the bed. The word *Master* printed on the apron made him entertain all sorts of ideas on what he might allow her to be the master of.

"Over easy or sunny-side up?"

Colin allowed his mouth to curve into a slow, suggestive smile. "Any which way I can get you."

She pointed the spatula at him. "You have a very dirty mind, Dr. McKenna."

"That's because you bring out the best in me." He waggled his brows, completely aware that another part of his anatomy was making its thoughts known on the subject and that Lucky hadn't missed that fact. "Or should I say beast?"

He started to get up, to pull her back into bed and the hell with breakfast, but she quickly turned around, laughing as she ran for the kitchen.

Colin chuckled then sat back down, watching as her delectable bare ass disappeared back into the kitchen.

He shook his head, having a hard time reconciling the playful, provocative woman of this morning with the closed-off, defensive woman from the night before.

Ignoring how badly he needed to use the bathroom, and how badly he wanted to follow after Lucky, he lay back on the bed and stared at the ceiling, trying to superimpose the latest picture of Lucky on top of the one she'd presented last night when he'd repeatedly prompted her for the reason why she hadn't used his key.

He hadn't received the answer; she'd given him a reason.

He absently rubbed the stubble covering his chin. He couldn't help feeling that there were a few things Lucky wasn't sharing with him, and not just because she wouldn't use his key.

He forced himself up and off the bed, stepped into the connecting master bath, then braced himself against the wall with one hand as he aimed his stiff member toward the toilet with the other.

It had been a long, long time since he'd spent this much time with a woman. Since Amanda, actually. He grinned, thinking his ex-fiancée wouldn't have been caught dead wearing the apron and nothing else, and wondering what she would make of another woman wearing it.

Lucky...

Lucky's mere presence seemed to brighten everything she touched. A man given to routine, he gladly interrupted his schedule in order to accommodate her.

But was she giving him the same consideration? Or was he, as he was coming to expect, a momentary distraction for her?

Ten minutes later, showered, shaved and dressed in his tennis whites, he found Lucky in the kitchen. He frowned when he discovered she'd changed from the apron into her clothes. She buttered whole wheat toast, her sensual expression making him think of everything but food.

Finishing up, she brushed the crumbs from her hands then pointed toward one of the two chairs at the island. "Sit."

Colin raised a brow as he did. "Who knew you were so bossy?"

She brushed against his back as she put a plate of eggs, bacon and homemade hash browns in front of him. ''Are you interested in seeing how bossy I can be?''

Colin always seemed to be in various stages of arousal whenever he was around Lucky—hell, even when he thought about her—and right now an erection tented the front of his shorts.

He heard her soft laughter in his ear before he felt her tongue along the outer shell. ''Looks like you're not the only one who's hungry.''

He reached for her and she easily stepped out of range, smiling as she filled a glass with orange juice then added it to the place setting in front of him.

Only then did he notice there was only one setting.

She leaned in and kissed him on the cheek. ''I've got to run.''

Colin knew a disappointment so complete that he felt like a kid whose favorite toy had just been taken away.

''Where?'' he found himself asking, wincing at the slight whine he heard in his voice.

She hugged him from behind and laughed softly. ''To work, of course.''

She kissed the back of his neck then released him.

"I'll see you later?" he asked, again sounding a little too needy for his liking.

"You'll see me later."

And just like that his apron angel left him sitting alone in the kitchen, his hard-on rivaling the dried Italian sausage hanging in its casing over the island.

11

"OH, YOU'VE got it bad."

Colin sat back in the lounge chair on Will's first-floor balcony and stretched his feet out to rest on top of the stone railing. He folded his hands behind his neck and grinned at his unhappy friend across the glass table from him.

"You've got it real bad," Will concluded.

"No, buddy," Colin disagreed. "I think what you meant to say is that I've got it good. Real good."

And he did. Mostly because when he had finished breakfast and walked back through the living room he'd noticed his apartment key was gone from the coffee table. At first he'd thought Lucky had moved it. But a brief look around had told him it wasn't just gone from the table, it was gone.

And he liked that.

Something resembling a growl came from his friend's direction.

Colin chuckled. "I take it that means your new girl from the hospital is sticking to her no-nookie-until-her-wedding-night promise?"

"You take correctly. In fact, I wish you could take it literally."

Will had played like a man dealing with plenty of pent-up sexual frustration on the tennis court today, growing further frustrated still when Colin refused to rise to the challenge.

"Your Lucky wouldn't happen to have any friends, now, would she?"

"And what would your girl have to say?"

"She's not my girl," Will said vehemently. "She won't be my girl until we sleep together. *Sleep* not being the operative word." He flopped back in his chair. "I mean, this is such a load of horse crap. It's not like she's a virgin. She freely admits that she's slept with her share of guys before."

"Ah, a born-again virgin. Dangerous, those types."

"What do you know of it?"

Colin held his hands up in surrender. "Whoa, buddy, looks like you could do with a bottle of oil and a porn mag. The sooner the better."

Will cursed under his breath, something Colin always found amusing when combined with his proper accent. "I haven't masturbated since I was fifteen years old, for Christ's sake."

Colin cocked a brow. "Really?"

"Yes, really. Since then there's always been one willing female or another to take care of those needs for me."

The midday summer sun was beginning to hit the edge of the balcony. Colin took his feet down from the railing. "And you say I'm the one who's got it bad. Sounds like *bad* is exactly the word for what you've got."

Will shook his head, then began nodding, as if torn between which expression was the right one. "I swear, if I don't get some soon, I'm going to explode."

Colin heard the main door of the building open and close, then he idly watched two young women in skimpy bikinis walk by on the path below the balcony, likely heading for the complex pool.

Will grumbled again. "Then you have her and the other one..."

"Who?"

Will jerked an arm toward the women. "The one in the green swimsuit. I've been going crazy thinking about her and her roommate in bed together right above me every night.'' He was heartily shaking his head. ''This morning I think my sheets were wet.''

Colin made a face. ''That's something I could have gone without knowing.''

''Tough. I've got to put up with you being late for our tennis date because of some floozy who's good in bed—''

''Lucky is not a floozy.''

''You're missing my point.''

''That's because I don't think you have one.''

''My point is,'' Will said, sitting forward as if getting ready to tell a patient he had a progressive, malignant form of cancer and had no more than a week to live, ''you're getting some and I'm not.''

''And you don't like that.''

Will pointed at him. ''Exactly!''

Colin picked up a towel from the table and tossed it at his friend. ''Come on, Casanova, let's go get cleaned up and get something in your stomach before you melt into a puddle of quivering hormones.''

''What? It's only eleven.''

''And I have an appointment at twelve-thirty.''

''Oh, you're just full of all kinds of good news

today, aren't you?'' Will glowered. ''I take it it's with her.''

''I wish. But, no. This appointment is with my attorney.''

''Your attorney? I don't know of any attorneys who keep weekend hours.''

''Yes, well, my attorney does.''

''Bully for you.''

Colin walked back inside the apartment and waited for his friend to follow.

COLIN FOUND himself whistling an hour and a half later as he left his place after a shower and a change of clothes. He glanced at his watch. He had five minutes to get to his attorney's office in the nearby Spitzer Building. He thought about walking the distance then remembered his workouts this morning—and last night—and decided he needed to conserve his energy for Lucky later.

Earlier he'd parked at the curb for easier access, so when he now exited the front of the building he pressed the button for the door lock release. He was shrugging into the suit jacket he was holding when he got a look at his car.

Not so much at his car but at what somebody had done to it.

On the side facing him, he saw a long key mark

engraved from the back bumper to the front. His gaze dropped down to the tires to find them slashed down to the rims. Colin's adrenaline level kicked up a notch as he looked around, spotting nothing and no one out of place. He crouched down to inspect the damage to the front tire, then looked under the car to find the same attention had been given to the other side.

Jamie.

It had to be.

He stood up and fished his cell phone out of his pants pocket. "Jack?" he said when his attorney picked up. "You're not going to believe this…"

ACROSS TOWN Lucky was walking back to work after making a run for lunch munchies. She was crunching chips from an open bag she held when she spotted something wrong with her car. The strip mall parking lot was crammed full of cars and hers was caught between a large SUV and a customized van. Across the back in red spray paint was written the word *Whore*.

Her mouth dried up, making it a chore to swallow the potato chips she'd barely chewed. Dropping the remainder of the chips into the grocery bag, she neared the old Chevy, the smell of fresh paint assaulting her nose. She couldn't remember if she'd looked at the car when she'd gone on the store run.

Rounding to the driver's side, she read more words. *He's my man.*

Her heart started pounding in her chest as she backed up and rounded the other side. *Stay home!*

Lucky rubbed her finger against the *S* in *Stay* and it came back with her paint-covered skin.

Her gaze shot to the mirrored windows of the van next to her. Could the person who had done this be in there watching her?

A woman holding shopping bags stepped between the two vehicles without acknowledging her then got into the van and drove away.

Lucky stood stunned for several minutes, then made her way back to the driver's side. She realized that the words hadn't been placed randomly. Rather she guessed they were meant to be read as a sentence.

He's my man, whore, stay home!

"Lucky?"

She heard Renae's voice but really didn't register it.

"What's the…holy shit."

Renae stopped next to her, taking in the graffiti that stood out like a police siren on a dark night.

"Jesus, who the hell would do something like this?"

Renae fished her cell phone out of her pocket and dialed 911, then disconnected. She picked up Lucky's right hand. "Are you hurt?"

Lucky shook her head. "It's from the paint."

"It's still wet? Good. Maybe we can rub out the worst of it before it dries. Here, give me your bag. I'm going to go get some towels. You stand here and wait for the police."

Lucky nodded, feeling as if her tongue had grown to twice its normal size in her mouth.

Who would do something like this? She tried to remember if Colin had mentioned anything about another woman. An old girlfriend. Any trouble he'd had in the past. Then her mind homed in on what had happened during their second encounter in his office. She'd been a breath away from finding out how well he would fill her when he'd grabbed her jaw and demanded to know whether someone named Jamie had put her up to the seduction.

She hadn't questioned him then. There really hadn't been any reason to. They hadn't had a relationship and she'd barely known him.

But she knew him now, didn't she? And he had never told her who Jamie was.

It seemed she wasn't the only one keeping secrets.

"JAMIE ISN'T an old girlfriend, Lucky. He's an ex-patient."

Hours later, back at Colin's place, after he'd told her his car had also been targeted at around the same time as hers, Colin answered her questions as directly as he could.

"He?" Lucky repeated. "The person who did this is a guy?"

"Yes. An ex-patient is suing me in civil court for sexual indecency."

She was looking at him closely. He knew the instant she put two and two together because her beautiful green eyes widened. "That's why you were so careful with me in the beginning."

Colin felt as if his grimace went all the way down to his bones. "Yes, that's why. Although by all rights I should have been anyway."

The apartment was quiet, both of them sitting in the kitchen at the island counter drinking coffee.

"Did you have an affair with him?" Lucky asked.

Colin squinted at her. "What?"

She shrugged. "It's a legitimate question."

"Maybe to you. But not to me." He was suddenly agitated. If he couldn't convince Lucky that he'd made no improper advances toward Jamie, what were his chances in convincing a judge if it came down to that.

"Look, Colin, you don't have to be gay to be curious."

"Trust me, if something had happened between Jamie and me, I would be the first to own up to it."

She smiled and reached out to cover his hand with hers. "I know."

Colin felt some of the tension drain from him.

"So what do the police say?"

Therein lay the rub, didn't it? "They said there's no evidence the two incidents are connected."

"Oh, both our cars just happened to be randomly vandalized?"

"That's about the thrust of it."

She was shaking her head.

"Look, Lucky, I'd like to pay to replace your car."

She stared at him as if he'd just told her he'd

been the one to paint the offensive words on her car. "You're joking, right?"

He shook his head. "No, I'm not. It's my fault this happened. I want to do the right thing."

"And the right thing would be to buy me a new car?"

He grinned at her. "Yes."

She laughed, although there was something a little dark in her eyes. "It was spray paint, Colin. Not a wrecking ball."

He shrugged. "You need a new car anyway so—"

"I don't need a new car. There's nothing wrong with the one I've got. As for the paint, Renae and I rubbed off a lot of it. And I called a repair shop and they said they could probably spot-paint over the rest." She reached for the cream, her movements a little jerky. "I think you should be more worried about your own car. Those key marks are deep."

"My insurance will take care of those."

A tense silence settled over the room. Colin opened his mouth to continue making his case when Lucky held her hand up.

"Drop it, doc. I'm not letting you get me a car."

Colin sat back, his sails effectively deflated. He watched her tap her short, unpainted fingernails against her mug in an angry staccato then saw her knuckles whiten as she gripped the handle.

"You know I don't mean any harm, don't you?" he asked quietly, not understanding why she was getting so worked up.

"Do I?"

She immediately looked regretful so he knew her response had been a knee-jerk reaction.

He also realized she had just revealed something very important about herself.

"I'm sorry. Of course I know you don't mean any harm," she said quietly.

Colin knew she'd been sorry for her harsh comment but was surprised by her one-eighty.

"But I don't want your help, Colin. Really, I don't."

"But what if I want to help you?"

She smiled at him. "Every time you want to help me, put an extra few dollars into the cup of the next homeless guy you come across." She stared into her mug. "Trust me, that'll be much easier for you than bringing this subject up with me again."

He narrowed his eyes. "You know, I don't get you," he thought aloud.

She reached out for his mug then pushed both of them off to the side of the counter. She scooted to sit on top and he leaned back so she could settle in front of him with her legs on either side. "Trust me, doc, it's all by design."

Colin's blood began a slow simmer that turned into a quick flash fire when she hiked up her skirt to reveal she wasn't wearing panties.

He swallowed hard as he laid his hands on her supple thighs, his thumbs pointed toward home base. "Have I ever told you that you have a hell of a way of changing the topic?"

She smiled and linked her hands together behind his neck, tugging him forward so she could kiss him. "Mmm. All the time." She leaned her head to the right, then the left, leisurely kissing him. "And I keep telling you that no topic is more important than this."

Colin wholeheartedly disagreed, but he wasn't up to telling her that just now. Not when his thumbs hit home and he found her hot and slick and ready for him.

But rather than looking for penetration, he pushed her so she was lying back down on the counter, then bent to taste the evidence of her need of him.

Five minutes, involving heated panting and a screaming orgasm, later he was about to pick her up to take her back to his room and his supply of condoms when he paused and stared down into her face.

''Why?'' he asked, his fingers cupping her bare bottom almost roughly. ''Why won't you let me see the real you, Lucky?''

A shadow so dark, so enormous, appeared in her vivid green eyes it nearly stole the air from his lungs. ''Nothing personal, Colin, but it's been so long that I don't even know who the real me is anymore.'' She leaned her head against his shoulder then kissed his neck. ''Just let it rest, okay? And trust me.''

As Colin picked her up and walked toward his bedroom at the other side of the apartment, he didn't know what to think. The simple truth of the matter was he didn't think Lucky trusted herself. And if she couldn't trust herself, how could he trust her?

12

THE FOLLOWING Monday, Colin sat back and listened as his attorney laid out the facts for him.

"Look, Colin, I wish there was some way to connect the events happening around you lately. But we have no solid proof to say Jamie is behind anything."

Colin fisted his hand where it lay in his lap. After the car incidents on Saturday, Don Maddox had agreed to move their appointment to that morning before he was due in court. But given that the prominent attorney was distracted at best, irritated with him at worst, the meeting was not going exactly as Colin had hoped it would. As an old friend of his father, Don was the first person he'd thought to turn to when Jamie Polson had sent him the original intent to sue. Don had managed to convince him that this was better than Jamie filing a formal complaint with the police, because that would have opened the case up to the public.

He was beginning to wonder if he shouldn't look elsewhere for an attorney.

"But you believe he is," he asked Maddox. "Behind what's happening, that is."

"What I believe or don't believe bears no relevance here." Don sighed heavily then looked at his watch. "I have to be in court in a little over an hour, so let's go over what I wanted to talk to you about."

He opened a file on his desk, then turned it so Colin could view the contents. An eight-by-ten-inch glossy photograph of him and Lucky at the restaurant last week leapt out at him.

He picked it up, shocked to see the moment caught on film. In the shot he was leaning forward talking to her while under the table she was rubbing her bare toes against his ankle.

"I thought we agreed you'd keep a low profile when it came to your, um, social activities," Maddox said, his chair squeaking as he reached for his coffee cup.

Anger, sure and swift, roared through Colin as he thumbed through the remainder of the shots. Him at Women Only. Lucky entering the outer doors of his apartment building. Lucky sitting in the waiting room of his office. "Where did you get these?" he demanded.

"They were couriered over last Friday. Thus the reason I asked on Saturday to meet with you today." He stared at Colin over the edge of his coffee cup. "So you understand my concern?"

"I understand that I'm being held hostage by a egomaniacal ex-patient who feels spurned because I didn't return his feelings."

Don shook his head. "You're still not getting it, are you?" The older man leaned forward, folding his hands on his desktop. "Colin, in cases like these the truth is a secondary consideration. We've talked about this. The damage to your career, your reputation, if this suit goes public…it will be irreparable."

"I don't care. File the countersuit." He closed the file and pushed it back across the desk.

One of the options all along was to answer Jamie's claims with a countersuit alleging libel and willful tort. Don had managed to talk him out of it so far, mostly with a lot of counseling from Colin's own father. But it was long past time for him to make a stand. Take some kind of action.

"I haven't been able to live my life since Jamie started all this bullshit and I'm tired of it," he told Don.

The seasoned attorney didn't blink. "And you think countersuing and taking this into the courts is going to end it quickly? Or how about your being tried in the court of public opinion? Even if criminal charges aren't brought, and you win your suit, do you think your partners want to be associated with someone who's been accused of improper sexual conduct against not only a patient, but a male patient?''

Colin winced. The older attorney's reasoning had managed to sand off the sharp edge of his anger.

But the anger was still there.

And, damn it, he intended to do something about it.

LUCKY SAT in the reception area of Colin's office waiting for his associate Dr. Morgan Szymanski to welcome in her and the other three members of her group for their session. She leafed through the few pages she'd written in her journal. Mostly she'd recorded random thoughts, things the therapist might want to see, like her feelings on alcohol and the consumption of it before getting behind the wheel of a car.

But on a couple of occasions she'd actually begun to write about those items of the most concern to her. First and foremost Colin McKenna.

She'd had enough forethought not to include

his name in the writings. But even she could tell the difference in her handwriting when she'd begun sharing her relationship with Colin, for example, thoughts about his offering up the key to his apartment. While the loops and swirls were neat in other areas, they all but disappeared when the topic turned to Colin, her mind no longer on how she was writing but rather on what she was writing.

She wished the passages were limited to a page or two so she might tear them out, but the thoughts were interspersed with the other entries and would take extensive rewriting, something she didn't have time for right now, even if she was moved to try.

She glanced at the closed door, wondering if she should take the journal out to her car and leave it there, then pretend she'd forgotten to bring it.

The problem lay in that there was already enough friction between her and the female psychologist. She didn't want to invite more. Not when her driver's license and possible probation hung in the balance.

"Good morning, Dr. McKenna."

Lucky's heart hiccupped in her chest as the receptionist greeted Colin. He was entering from the outer door, obviously just arriving at the office or perhaps returning from an appointment.

And looking none too happy to be there.

He hadn't spotted her yet and she took the opportunity to note the deep grooves on either side of his mouth and his stern expression.

When she'd left him a few hours ago he'd been grinning and happy and oh so sexily disheveled. What had happened since then?

He accepted a handful of messages from the receptionist then turned toward his office, his gaze immediately falling on her. He blinked and she smiled, expecting him to return it.

Instead his grimace deepened further as if she was not only the last person he expected to see, but the last one he wanted to see.

"Okay, I think we're a go."

Lucky glanced at where Dr. Szymanski had opened her office door. She began getting up along with her other three group members.

Colin briefly closed his eyes and she thought she heard him utter a mild curse. "Miss Clayborn?" he asked before she disappeared into the other office. "If you have a few moments after your appointment, I'd like to have a word with you in my office."

She smiled at him, but the expression somehow

didn't make it below the surface. "Sorry, Dr. Mc-Kenna, but I have to get to work straight after."

His eyes narrowed then he nodded. "Very well then."

Lucky glanced at the receptionist, who was listening to the exchange with open interest, then followed the rest of her group mates into the office and closed the door behind her.

LATER THAT AFTERNOON Colin had his elbows planted on his desktop and the telephone receiver held to his ear. He absently rubbed his closed eyelids, wondering how one day could seem so endlessly long.

Lucky hadn't stopped by his office following her session with Morgan earlier, just as she'd said she wouldn't. He had hoped she would change her mind and duck in for a moment, if only so he could apologize to her. Although he supposed he couldn't blame her. Had she looked at him the way he was sure he had looked at her when he'd first spotted her in the reception area, he wouldn't have wanted to see her so soon afterward, either.

He blew out the long breath that filled his cheeks and sat back hard in his chair, the memory of the photographs his attorney had shown him shifting through his mind. It seemed that not only

was Jamie not giving up, as he and Don had
hoped he would, he was upping the ante.

Were he and Lucky at physical risk? He
couldn't be sure. But he wasn't about to sit back
and wait to see if there was even a chance that
spray-painted cars and slashed tires might turn
into something more serious, something more
dangerous.

"Mr. McKenna? I can do it," Jenny Mathena
came back on the line. "But you have to know
that given the accelerated time frame you've
given me it's going to take cash and lots of it—"

"Money's no object."

Barely a pause, then, "Very good then. I'll be
in touch. Possibly as soon as tomorrow."

"Thanks, Miss Mathena."

"It's Jenny, please."

Colin broke the connection soon afterward,
then sat staring at the wall displaying his license
to practice and his diplomas. Finally he got up
and collected his briefcase and jacket, feeling
more hopeful now than he had all day—in fact,
than he had in a good long while.

During the drive home he opened his windows
instead of switching on the air-conditioning, em-
bracing the signs of summer rather than rejecting
them. He didn't know how Don Maddox would

feel about what he was doing, but the older attorney wasn't going to find out unless and until Colin got results.

He parked his repaired car in the underground garage of the building then rode the elevator up to his apartment. Immediately the elevator door opened, the smell of something cooking assaulted his nose. Usually he couldn't tell what the other tenants were having for dinner. He unlocked the apartment door and discovered that the scent wasn't emanating from another apartment but rather from his own.

Lucky had used his key.

He stood reflecting on the many implications of her actions. She'd so vehemently and mysteriously rejected the idea when he'd originally suggested it. Now she'd gone ahead and used it on her own. Did it mean something more than that she'd wanted to cook him dinner? Or was it a simple matter of control and that she needed to be the one to decide when to use the key?

Either way, he was glad she was here.

He quietly put his briefcase down on the floor and hung up his jacket then rounded the corner to peer into the kitchen. Lucky was wearing a pair of snug white shorts and a clingy black tank, which softly emphasized her provocative curves.

Colin leaned against the jamb and crossed his arms, enjoying the sight she made from behind as she stirred something in one pan then added spaghetti to another. Her feet were gloriously bare and her hair was tied into a loose knot at her shoulders. She was summer and its sultry heat wrapped up into one irresistible package.

Something warm made its way through Colin's bloodstream. Something that had nothing to do with sex and everything to do with…love.

He swallowed hard. The sound must have been loud enough for Lucky to hear because she swiveled around to face him, the wooden spoon she held dripping red sauce on the black-and-white tile of the floor.

"Oh!" she said, quickly putting her other hand under the spoon. "I didn't hear you come in."

He grinned, watching as she moved the spoon to the sink then rinsed the sauce from her hands. Colin grabbed a paper towel and crouched to the floor at the same time she did to wipe up the spot. The position put him exactly where he wanted to be: face-to-face with Lucky.

He looked into her flushed face, his gaze taking in every familiar feature. Then he kissed her, nearly knocking her back on her heels. She smiled at him. "Where did that come from?"

"Hmm…I don't know. But there's lots more if you want it."

She smiled at him in that way that made his stomach tighten and his arousal stir. "Mmm. A man with a one-track mind. I like that."

Colin kissed her again, lingering there against her lush lips. Rather than a man with a one-track mind, the train in his head had come into the station a while ago and was now facing myriad other tracks. And he wanted to explore all of them with this amazing woman.

She pulled away and laughed. "You sure know how to sweep a girl off her feet."

"Then let me help you back onto your feet." He easily got up and held his hand out, helping her to stand in front of him.

"I hope you like spaghetti," she said, turning back to the stove.

"I love spaghetti."

Was it him or was there a stiffness about her?

"There's a bottle of wine breathing on the counter over there. Pour us a couple of glasses?"

He did and handed her one.

"Thanks," she said, taking a sip.

She seemed to be extraordinarily interested in what she was doing on the stove.

Of course. Kissing her nearly had made him forget their run-in outside his office.

Colin leaned against the counter next to the stove. "About this morning," he said quietly. "I'm sorry I reacted the way I did when I saw you. I'd just met with my attorney and was distracted. I'd forgotten it was your day with Morgan."

She stirred the spaghetti with a fork. "So you thought I'd stopped by to see how I could heat things up?"

He reached for a lock of her hair, rubbing the silken strands against his skin. "Mmm."

He debated telling her what had happened at Maddox's, but felt that doing so would be akin to offering up an excuse for his bad behavior. And he was never one for excuses. An apology was better.

"So how did everything go?" she asked, taking the spaghetti from the burner and turning the contents into a colander.

"With my attorney? Not so good."

She glanced at him while she ran cold water. "What happened?"

Colin ran his hand over his face.

She shut off the water and leaned her hips

against his. "Now look what I've gone and done. I've chased the grin from your face."

He smiled down at her and grasped her rounded hips.

"That bad, huh?" she asked.

He nodded.

"Let's not talk about it, then. It always makes things worse to talk about bad news."

Colin blinked at the classic signs of avoidance as she turned off the last burner then picked up a plate and began piling spaghetti on top. "Tell me when."

He did, only he found himself wishing he could say "when" to her.

This cat-and-mouse game they were playing with their relationship was beginning to wear on his nerves. He didn't like not knowing what was going on in her head. He didn't like not knowing what resided in her heart.

Within moments they were both seated at the kitchen island instead of the formal dining-room table in the other room. Lucky opened the foil-wrapped garlic bread she'd taken out of the oven.

"Lucky...tell me something about yourself," he asked quietly. "Your hopes, your dreams. What you were like growing up. Tell me something no one else knows about you."

He watched as she seemed to have a hard time swallowing.

"Did you want to talk about what happened with your attorney?" she asked.

"No. This isn't about me. This is about you."

That casual atmosphere took a very chilly nose-dive and there was nothing Colin could do to change that.

"So we're back to that again," Lucky whispered, pushing spaghetti around her plate without eating it. "Look, Colin, I don't come here to delve into the past, to examine every aspect of my life under the light of a microscope trying to figure out why this happened or how I might have been able to circumvent that. I come here to forget."

"But you can't, can you?"

She grasped her wineglass and took a long sip.

"Whatever you're running from...it's starting to find you here, too, isn't it?"

13

MUCH LATER that night Colin jerked awake and pushed up to lean his weight against his elbows. What was that? He glanced around his darkened bedroom, not sure if it was something in his dream that had awakened him or a sound in the apartment.

He glanced at the empty spot next to him, then tossed the top sheet from his waist and sat up.

Tonight had not gone the way he'd planned. In fact the entire day had seemed to play out slightly off-kilter. But he'd counted it as a good sign that Lucky hadn't left when he'd pressed her for answers during dinner earlier that night. He hadn't made any headway into understanding what made her tick, but perhaps he'd made a small dent in her armor.

And armor was exactly what it was, wasn't it? Not just one simple reason why she welcomed him between her thighs yet kept him away from her heart. Whatever was behind Lucky's behavior ran deep and had damaged her to an extent he could only guess at.

He rubbed the sleep from his face. Sometimes it sucked being a psychiatrist. He couldn't look at someone without wanting to know what had made them into the person they were.

He couldn't look at Lucky without wanting to possess her fully, heart, mind and soul.

He glanced toward the empty bathroom then put on his boxers and stepped into the living room. A sweep of the kitchen and the rest of the large penthouse showed no sign of her. It was only when he walked back into the living room that he spotted one of the French doors slightly open, the sheer curtains billowing in the light breeze.

He pulled back the gauzy fabric and opened the door farther, immediately spotting Lucky sitting on the marble tile of the balcony, her back against the wall of glass, the remainder of the bottle of wine from dinner next to her along with a single glass. She didn't seem to be aware that he'd joined her. She merely sat staring sightlessly out across the Maumee River.

But she was still here.

As he took her in, from the way her shoulders

slumped, to the sadness on her face, he grabbed onto that thought and held it close.

She was still here....

LUCKY KNEW the moment Colin had joined her. But she was slightly foggy from the wine and the enormity of her thoughts and couldn't seem to make herself respond. Not to sit up straighter. Not to greet him in some way. Not even to acknowledge his presence.

He pulled a chair out from the large glass table positioned a short distance away and sat down, his body angled toward hers. He didn't say anything. And she was glad for that.

Lucky closed her eyes and stretched her neck to accommodate her hard swallow. She was thirty years old and had long ago gotten used to the cycles of her life. Despite what the court thought, liquor was not her drug of choice, sex was. And the better the sex, the more successful she was at keeping her many demons at bay.

But the instant the excitement associated with sex began to wane, when she either grew bored or the guy started asking too many questions, started making commitment noises, she was out the door, the latest cycle complete.

And that's when liquor entered in. A little

something to tide her over until she met the next guy.

Only this time the cycle had come full circle sooner than it ever had before.

And it wasn't because the sex had lost its appeal—if anything, the heights she achieved with Colin were higher than she'd ever reached before. It wasn't because she was bored—Colin fascinated her on so many levels that he emerged somewhat like a Christmas present with an infinite number of smaller presents wrapped inside.

And it wasn't even because he had started making commitment noises.

No, this time the cycle was different.

Because this time she'd fallen in love.

She reached for the wine bottle and poured the last bit into her empty glass. But she didn't drink it. Instead she nudged the glass around by the base on the tile, watching the contents swirl around. She was as numb as she was going to get, which was not numb at all. She had the sneaking suspicion that no amount of alcohol was going to make her all right this time around.

''I can't have children,'' she said into the dark night.

She blinked, unaware that she'd said the words aloud until she heard them.

There was no response for a long time, making her wonder if her mind was playing tricks on her, if the wine was making her imagine things.

''I'm sorry,'' finally came Colin's soft response.

She slowly turned to look at him, her head still resting against the glass door behind her. ''Why are you sorry? I made the conscious decision not ever to have children.''

He squinted at her. ''So what you're saying is that you don't want kids.''

''No. What I'm saying is that I can't have kids. I paid for a tubal ligation when I was nineteen.''

Any other man might have looked at her strangely. But not Colin. While curiosity and concern painted his handsome features, he didn't judge her for her actions. He merely accepted her.

And, curiously enough, didn't question her.

She gave a small, sad smile. After all the questioning he'd done in the past week, it was ironic that he wasn't asking any questions now. Was it because he knew she was ready to tell him herself? Or having caught a glimpse of what she'd kept hidden for so long, was he afraid of what she might reveal?

''I've never known you to drink,'' he said quietly.

She looked at the glass she was still toying with. "Funny, don't you think, considering that's the entire reason we met?" She cleared her throat. "The reason you haven't seen me drink until now is that I haven't needed to drink."

"But you need to now."

She looked at him. "Yes."

DESPITE HER WORDS, Colin had yet to watch Lucky take a sip from the glass since he'd joined her on the balcony. Oh, he was aware that the bottle was empty. But he felt a burst of gratitude that she wasn't chugging down what remained in her glass then going in search of something else inside the penthouse to blur her pain with.

And pain is exactly what he saw written all over her. From her beautiful face and the uncaring way she held her body to the dark shadow in her eyes, it was obvious this woman had been hurt and hurt deeply in the past. And that hurt had never gone away.

He clasped his hands tightly between his knees, considering her surprising desire never to have children and the actions she'd taken to make sure she never would. He knew of few doctors who would agree to perform the surgery on a nineteen-year-old. Which further emphasized the severity of her reasons for having done it.

Children. Yes, he admitted, he wanted them. At least two. As an only child, he'd always wondered what it would have been like to have a sibling. And depending on the soundness of his career after Jamie got done with him, he might like to have three or four mini McKennas running around the place.

The thought that there was no chance of having them with Lucky twisted his stomach in a way that went beyond physical pain.

It was then he realized that despite the appearance of their relationship being strictly sexual, he'd secretly begun imagining a future with Lucky, a future that included weddings and baptisms and Christmases spent in front of a roaring fire.

An undetermined future Lucky had the power to give him...or take away from him.

The chair he sat in squeaked as he leaned back. He'd never been this close emotionally to somebody this damaged before. No, he didn't know the details behind her pain, but he'd suspected from the beginning that Lucky was different. He'd kidded himself into thinking she was just more of a free spirit, more sexual. And while almost everyone had his or her neuroses, Lucky didn't have a fear of heights or of commitment or of touching objects like doorknobs that somebody else might have put their germs on or anything like that.

Rather he sensed her problems were not ones that could be fixed with a year's worth of therapy. No. Hers would take an entire lifetime to address, and still she might not ever come close to fixing them.

"Do you want to know why I became a psychiatrist?" he said quietly into the dark.

She didn't say anything and he was afraid either she hadn't heard him or had decided not to respond. Then, finally, she looked at him, her glorious long hair shifting on the smooth glass behind her. "Because you grew up in a dysfunctional family and wanted to save the world?"

He smiled faintly at that. "Because I couldn't stand the sight of blood."

She blinked at him.

"That's right. The very first day of my residency at St. V's, a patient with an arterial wound was wheeled into emergency—the type of wound that if not immediately addressed can cause death in less than fifteen minutes. Essentially the patient bleeds to death." He looked out at the waters of the Maumee. "When I released the tourniquet and blood spurted across my neck and the front of my smock, I choked. I couldn't move.''

He remembered standing there completely frozen as the other staff moved efficiently and quickly around him, unaware of his dilemma. Will, who was doing his residency at the same hospital and happened to be on with him that day, had caught onto what was happening and stepped in to see to the patient. His friend had been completely unaffected by the thick, red substance coating his arms and gloves.

Colin hated to think of what might have happened if Will hadn't taken charge.

''It was your first day,'' Lucky said quietly.

He looked at her. ''It only got worse from there.'' He rubbed the heel of his hand against his brow. ''So what becomes of a doctor who can't hack it in the emergency room?''

''He becomes a shrink?''

He laughed softly, marveling at her attempt at humor given her precarious emotional state. ''That's exactly what he does.''

The sound of a plane passing overhead, moving in the direction of the Toledo Airport some twenty miles outside of town, caught his attention. Colin watched the blinking lights as it passed, then stared at the sliver of moon seemingly suspended in the sky by a string.

"My father was a doctor. A surgeon."

Lucky's words surprised him. Given what he'd seen of her, the jobs she held, the way she lived, he'd guessed she'd come from simpler means.

Of course she'd never offered up information to dispel that image. But he still felt chagrin at his incorrect snap judgment of her.

"And your mother?"

She finally picked up the glass, stared into it, then swallowed the contents. "She died of pancreatic cancer when I was fourteen."

Colin stiffened. She'd revealed more about herself in the past half hour than she had in the past three weeks. And while he was grateful for the insight into her past, he couldn't help the feeling that it was just a glimpse. That the wounds she bore went deeper still.

"I'm sorry," he said.

Such ineffectual words. But the only words he had.

She nodded.

And just like that Colin felt the connection between them snap.

Lucky pushed to her feet, picked up the bottle and glass and turned to face him. If she hadn't needed him to move in order to pass, he suspected she would already have been inside.

"Excuse me," she said quietly.

Colin looked up at her shadowy face from where he still sat in the chair. Considered the even larger shadows that resided within her.

"No."

The word was simple but meaningful. Whatever had started tonight had to continue tonight. He wasn't going to give up that easily.

Lucky began to try to pass and he gently grasped her wrists, forbidding her passage.

"Please, Lucky," he pleaded with her softly. "Tell me what's causing you so much pain."

The unmistakable glisten of tears in her eyes made his chest tighten.

"Let me go," she whispered, her body going rigid. "Please."

The problem with her request was that Colin feared she didn't mean just let her go now...but let her go for good.

And he couldn't do that.

"Please," she said again.

She jerked her arms to free herself and he strengthened his grasp. The wineglass slipped from her grip, breaking into scattered shards on the tile beneath their bare feet, shattering the silence of the night.

Colin swept her up into his lap, holding her so tightly he couldn't breathe. He took the bottle from her hands and put it on the table behind him.

"Please, please don't walk away from this, Lucky," he murmured into her ear through the fragrant cloud of her hair. "Please don't walk away from us."

She pushed against him, fighting hard. Fighting for everything she was worth.

And he held on just as tightly.

"There is no us," she said vehemently. "There's you…and there's me…and I'm done."

He grasped her chin and held her face in front of his, wildly searching her face. "You can't be. Because I won't let you."

She stared at him, the tears in her eyes sliding down over her dark lashes and streaking her cheeks.

"I love you, Lucky."

14

LUCKY WANTED to put her hands over her ears. Block out Colin's softly spoken words. Close her eyes and deny herself the luxury of seeing his handsome face. So full of warmth…so full of emotion…so full of love.

"No!" she whispered. "No, no, no!"

She pushed at him, battling as much against a primal something emerging from inside her, slashing at her heart, thundering through her veins, as she was struggling against him.

But the harder she fought, the tighter Colin held her in his arms.

"I love you, Lucky. I love you."

The words were what so many little girls dreamed about hearing from the man they would some day love. But they inspired nothing but darkness inside her. "Stop it! Stop saying that!"

Love you…love you…love you…

"Why, Lucky? Why should I stop saying it?" Colin pressed his lips against her wet cheek, the gentle gesture in sharp contrast to the way he restrained her. "It's how I feel."

Her throat was raw and tight. "What do you know about what you feel? What do any of us know about what we feel? Love is...love is just a word. A ridiculous, stupid little word we all pack so much meaning into, but in the end that's all it is. A word."

"A word that's caused you pain."

She stared at him, filled with the desire to kiss him and battle against him all at once. "Yes," she breathed, giving brief vent to the conflicting emotions roiling within her.

"Is it your mother, Lucky? Is it her death that hurt you?"

Her muscles tensed further. "My mother loved me. And I knew that, up to, including and even after the day that she died."

"Then someone else..."

Yes, very definitely someone else...

She continued struggling, but to no avail. Colin merely waited her out until exhaustion settled over her strained muscles like a heavy shadow. She was so tired of fighting. Not only Colin, but the demons she warred with every day. She went still, completely still, in the circle of his arms. But she didn't draw comfort from his embrace. Instead his arms were a makeshift prison cell designed to keep her from doing what she most wanted to do. Run.

"You know, I once thought it was written somewhere that parents are supposed to love their children," she heard a woman's voice say, a voice that sounded remarkably like hers. "A man, a woman, they get married. They set up house. A loving house in which to bring up a baby, maybe two or three." She swallowed hard, the thick gulp sounding loud in the quiet night. "And that was my life."

Silence for a long moment, then, "Until your mother died."

She stared at him, wishing it were lighter so she could see him better. "You think you know everything, don't you, Dr. McKenna?" she asked him softly. "You think you know how it feels to live in a house that was a warm and loving home one day, then overnight turned into nothing more than a collection of empty rooms devoid of laughter, of sunshine…of love. Rooms full of fear and unspoken threat."

"Your father didn't love you."

She trapped his gaze with hers, her eyes narrowing. "The problem wasn't that my father didn't love me. The problem was that after my mother died, my father loved me the wrong way.''

Her breath hitched in her throat as she dared him to say the words she couldn't. Dared him to try to take the conversation in another direction.

Instead he said, ''Oh, Jesus.''

Lucky had expected any response. Any response but the grief-filled, loving reaction Colin showed her.

He tightened his arms around her.

And she fought him.

Only she was no longer fighting against only him. She was battling against the barrage of acid memories from her past. Memories of coming home after school at fourteen, determined to keep her family together in the wake of her mother's death, and realizing that her father was looking at her in a different way. Staring at her in a strange, unsettling way that made her skin crawl and made her feel…dirty.

He was watching her in a way that a father shouldn't watch his own flesh and blood.

But still she plowed forward, hoping beyond hope that she was imagining the cause for the uneasiness she felt with each passing day. With the help of a housekeeper, she made sure dinner was on the table every night by six. That her father's newspaper was laid out on his home office desk, his slippers and remote by his easy chair.

And every night she'd bid him goodnight from the living-room doorway and hurry off to her room where she would lock herself inside until she would hear the housekeeper come in the following morning.

Still she couldn't help the foreboding that followed her like a dark shadow. She'd open the shower curtain after taking a shower and find her father standing there. Not offering her a towel and a loving smile as he had so many times when she was a child, but openly staring at her nude body, the expression on his face not one of fatherly love, but of twisted physical need. She'd wake in the middle of the night and hear him knocking on her door begging to talk to her and she would cower under the covers and pretend she didn't hear him, hot tears scalding her cheeks, waiting for him to go away.

She'd felt so terribly, utterly alone. The happy life and memories she'd once had crumbled in her hands the tighter she tried to hold on to them. The only person she had left in the world was the only one she couldn't turn to. One desperate afternoon she'd tried talking to the one person she thought she could trust, the only one who might be able to help. She reached out to her mother's sister, her aunt. And she'd received a stinging slap across the face for her efforts that still branded her heart. Her father was an important surgeon. He'd just lost his wife. How dare she utter such vile lies about him, her aunt had told her.

Devastated, she'd had little other choice but to go back and continue living in fear of her own father. And she had. For three long years. Keeping busy with school activities during the day, and hiding in the prison cell that was her bedroom at night, counting off the days until she left for college...and praying that tonight would be the night that he wouldn't come to her door and plead for her to let him in.

Then came the day where she was seventeen and she'd arrived home from school and found the locks removed from her bedroom door.

"Love," she whispered now, her heart pounding so hard against her ribcage she was afraid it might punch straight through. "My father said he loved me. Kept saying he loved me. Especially when he...he violated me in my childhood bed...across the hall from the room he used to share with my mother...in the house that had once been a beautiful home."

She stared at Colin.

"So don't you ever talk to me about love again, do you hear me? Because it doesn't exist. Not in any way that matters."

COLIN GAZED into Lucky's tear-streaked, pain-filled face, feeling as if she'd just told him night was day. That the moon had just been ripped from the sky.

He pulled her closer and she fought him, although not half as hard as she had earlier. Telling him what she had, baring herself so completely, had drained her.

And had spilled a permanent stain across his own heart.

He pressed his chin against the side of her head and said fervently, "What your father did to you, that was not love, Lucky."

A bitter, black fury filled him to overflowing toward the man who had hurt this unique and stunning creature. He knew a desire to inflict physical pain in a way he had never felt before. To do damage, to lash out on Lucky's behalf, to right what was so horribly, terribly wrong.

As he sat there holding her tightly, he felt so overwhelmingly helpless in the face of such pain that he didn't know what to say. What to do. Was incapable of doing anything more than merely hold her.

"I left the next day and I never went back," Lucky whispered, continuing with a story he no longer wanted to hear. That he wanted to block out as surely as she had tried to block it out for so many years.

Maybe she was right. Maybe talking about bad things sometimes only made them worse.

Fourteen years old. Still a child in so many ways. A girl who had lost her mother. Who needed the support of her father.

Professionally he'd dealt with countless cases similar to Lucky's. Heard the stories from the girls and guys at Crossroads. Knew the cold hard facts: one out of three girls and one out of five boys would not reach eighteen without being sexually molested in some way by a relative, neighbor or family friend.

But knowing about it and hearing about it from others was far different from learning it had happened to the one you loved.

His kneejerk reaction was visceral. All-encompassing. Vicious.

"Where is he now?" he asked, his jaw clenched so tight he heard it pop.

He tried to keep his expression neutral as Lucky searched his face.

"Why, Colin? So you can track him down? Make him pay for what he did to me?" She looked into his eyes then tried to free herself. Not in a jerky, overly emotional way as she had before. No, she seemed to have regained control over her emotions somewhat.

So he released her.

She got up and carefully stepped well to the left of the broken glass and to the wrought-iron railing.

"He's dead."

Colin stared at her back.

"He died almost a year to the day after I left. Suicide."

He felt as if he'd been physically slapped. All that anger. That pain. And no outlet for it. No closure. Because the man who could have given her that had taken it with him to his grave.

"I don't know how many times when I was out there by myself, working crappy part-time jobs and living in flophouses that I…that I wished him dead. Then just like that…he was."

"That's not your fault, Lucky." Neither was her father's twisted need for her.

She turned to face him, looking so somber, so

serious, so injured that he had a hard time reconciling her with the fun-loving woman he'd first
met. The devil-may-care woman who had so easily destroyed all of his barriers while keeping her
own carefully intact.

"I know that," she whispered. "But that
doesn't make living with myself any easier." He
noticed the way she tightly gripped the iron railing with her hands. "Despite everything, for the
fourteen years before my mother died, he was my
father. And I loved him."

He heard the grief in her voice. Grief for the
mother she had lost. The father who had betrayed
himself and her. Grief for the little girl who'd had
to grow up too fast.

"There's that damn word again. *Love.*"

"Lucky, I…"

When he fell silent and didn't finish his sentence, she looked up at him. "You what?"

"I'm…I'm sorry."

Those horribly inadequate words again.

"I'm sorry that the solid, loving foundation that
had formed so much of your early life was jerked
out from underneath you. I'm sorry that you were
denied the love and the security that every child
born on this earth deserves." He got up and went
to stand in front of her, not continuing until he

knew she was looking at him. Really looking at him. "I'm sorry that you've never known what real love is. Real adult love between a man and a woman."

She moved to pass him.

One last time he grasped her wrist. She stopped and he forced himself to release her, no matter the risk of flight.

He gazed at her, feeling love warm him to the core…and wishing he could pass it on to her like some sort of virus. "I can't erase your past, Lucky. I can't wave a magic wand and make it all go away, as much as I'd like to try." His heart pounded. "And I can't make you stay."

She didn't move.

"But I do want you to stay. If just for tonight. If just so I can hold you one more time."

She looked up at him, gratitude and, yes, love shining from her eyes, even if she didn't realize that's what she felt.

This time it was she who did the touching. She reached out and slid her fingers into his, then she kissed him, saying with her actions what her words denied.

LUCKY LAY against the soft sheets of Colin's bed, watching him as he gazed at her. The only sounds were the thick beating of her heart and the rustle of bedclothes as Colin moved. His touch as he stroked her body was so gentle, so tender, she felt tears collect in the back of her throat all over again.

He'd been wrong when he'd said he couldn't wave a magic wand and make it all go away. Because being with him made her think of nothing else but him. Of this. Of the thought of their bodies connecting in a way she'd never experienced with another man. Oh, sure, she might have been able to forget for a few precious moments before. And the pursuit of those diversions might have engaged her mind for brief periods.

But no one had ever touched her heart before.

And as Colin ran his hands slowly, almost reverently, down the sides of her arms and waist and thighs, he made her feel as if he was stroking her heart.

By design, she liked her sex fast and hard and spontaneous so she wouldn't have the chance to think about what she was doing. So she couldn't consider who she was, where she'd come from and where she was going from there. The moment of release was what she sought single-mindedly.

But as Colin set a slow, leisurely pace now, she found that while a restless energy filled her, it neither frightened her nor compelled her to speed things up. She was content to lie there, concentrate on her breathing, and process the ways his touch affected her.

His fingertips skimmed over her right nipple and shooting stars of sensation arced toward her sex. His light stubble rasped against her belly and she melted against the mattress, trembling with sweet awareness. He kissed her and she no longer felt like one individual person but rather a part of a union that not only felt right, but felt natural. Something bigger than her. Bigger than both of them.

He'd said he loved her. And while shadowy demons had crept out of the dark places in her heart to deny that love, now she allowed herself to feel it as surely as if the sentiment were a thick, velvety cloak that he'd gently tucked around her. Something tangible. Something that refused to be denied.

When his fingers would have touched the damp curls between her thighs, he hesitated, then pulled away, instead curving her body against his from behind and holding her. Merely holding her.

Lucky opened her mouth to protest, but he made a soft shushing sound.

"Lie still," he murmured. "Tonight I just want to hold you."

Unreleased sexual energy seemed to fill her to overflowing, but rather than act on it, she lay still, listening to the beat of her heart, his heart, and reveling in the feel of his skin against hers.

And before she knew it she was asleep.

15

THREE DAYS LATER, Colin sat at a stool at his kitchen island, alone, sipping coffee and pretending to read the paper. He'd gone for his morning run. He'd showered and changed. He'd eaten breakfast. And it was still only 7:00 a.m., the minutes on his watch seeming to pass with torturous slowness, a good hour to go before he had to be at the office.

He'd known when Lucky had left his apartment Tuesday morning that he might not see her again. But knowing that and living it were two completely different things. He'd worked on automatic pilot for the past few days, consulting clients, meeting with his attorney and running until his feet ached from pounding relentlessly against the cement walkway rimming the Maumee River, then in through the city, running not until he ran out of road, but until he couldn't physically take another step.

Despite his best efforts, still Lucky was with

him, the secret she had revealed clinging to him to like an unshakable shadow that refused to retreat even in the brightest light. He needed to see her, but held to the promise he'd made when she'd sweetly kissed him goodbye.

"Please," she'd said, searching his face. "Please give me some time alone to work through all this."

He'd wanted to tell her no. To try to convince her that he could help her. But he was afraid that the harder he tried to make things work, the more they wouldn't.

So he'd promised to give her the space that she needed.

If only he wasn't afraid that space would take her away from him forever.

Throughout his entire career he'd worked at helping others solve their problems, but with a great deal of remorse in the days since Lucky had shared her secret, he realized he'd never been *dedicated* to those same patients. Had never gone beyond the approaches he'd been taught, had never tried to implement new treatments or strategies. He'd gone with the flow, no more than a nine-to-five worker who looked forward to the end of the day, and planned what he would do outside work when he received his paycheck.

Even when it came to the kids at Crossroads, the runaways who needed the most help, he never visited more than once a month. He'd convinced himself that his being there, free of charge, every thirty days was enough. Patted himself on the back for being such a caring person, a humanitarian, not merely a therapist. But when all was said and done, his actions were small, merely a single cinder block against the overwhelming tide of need that would swell toward him if he reached out and unlocked the flood gates.

Of course now that he saw that, understood that, now that he was inspired to do more, do better, he couldn't help the person he wanted to help most in the world: He couldn't help Lucky.

Or could he?

He closed the paper, finally giving up on making any sense out of it, his mind catching on to the patterns that made up his own life.

In medical school, professional detachment had been drummed into him and his fellow students from day one. Words like *limitations* and *boundaries* had seen more emphasis than the words *compassion* and *dedication* and *do no harm*, which were outlined in the Hippocratic oath. After all, he had to protect and maintain and recognize his own personal borders. So when he faced patients like the Hansens, listened to their marital problems, and looked at his watch to tick off the minutes until the session was over, he excused himself for his indifference, telling himself there was only so much he could do.

His pattern of behavior was just as damning as Lucky's was. Possibly worse, because hers had been born of tragedy and pain while his stemmed from the detachment he'd been taught and had taken literally.

No, it was no longer detachment now, was it? Instead it had morphed into passivity and ignorance.

The people who sought his attention were at the ends of their ropes. If he didn't go the extra mile to help them hold on to it and give them the tools they needed to climb back up, what was he really doing but playing the role of sounding board?

The more he thought about the situation, the more agitated he became, and the greater the temptation to excuse himself grew.

But not this time. No. This time he was going to do something about it, one step at a time, one foot in front of the other. His wasn't a job that could be forgotten about the moment he walked out of the office at 5:00 p.m. He didn't work at a textile plant; he was being entrusted with people's lives. And it was long past time he began giving them the attention they not only needed, but deserved.

And maybe, just maybe, through them, through correcting his own ugly patterns, he would learn how to get through to Lucky.

LUCKY SPRAYED foam cleaner on the glass then in slow, lethargic circles ran a cloth over the front window of Women Only, her mind a million miles away. Her heart was across town, held tightly by a man she had resolved to pack away into the past, the way she had packed so much of her life.

Only Colin refused to be packed away. Not physically. Physically he hadn't contacted her, hadn't sought her out. And, she told herself, she was glad he hadn't. Happy he was staying true to his promise not to pursue her.

But still he was always there, lingering on the fringes of every thought, present with every beat of her heart.

Something significant had happened to her Monday night. Something she couldn't begin to explain. Something she feared she wouldn't completely understand even with twenty years of thought. But when she'd opened up the battered, weathered door to her past and let out the contents for Colin to see, the ghosts hadn't gone back into the closet. Instead they stood right in front of her, no longer looming as the undefeatable enemies she combated with sex and drink. Rather they seem to coalesce into one giant, oversized, ugly puppet, staring at her, waiting for her to tell it what to do.

And she had no idea what to instruct it.

And since that Monday night when she'd sat on Colin's balcony and drunk herself into a stupor before going stone-cold sober in the light of his refusal to let her run, she hadn't had a drop of alcohol. In fact, last night she'd thrown every last bottle hidden around her apartment into the garbage bin, then hauled it all out to the curbside where she'd stood and watched the city refuse collectors pick it up this morning.

She'd expected to feel panic at the sight. To be assailed with the desire to run out and replenish her supply.

Instead she'd felt…relief. Something akin to freedom. Or maybe not so much freedom. Instead it felt as if she'd ascended to a step from which the world looked slightly different from the reality she'd known for so long.

"Uh oh. Trouble in Lover Land."

Lucky blinked at the square foot of glass she had been rubbing for the past five minutes, then looked at Renae standing in the open doorway, her arms crossed, her smile bright as the morning sun.

Lucky offered up a genuine smile. Over the past week and a half, she'd become attached to Women Only, Renae and owner Ginger Wasserman and the other employees in a way she'd never allowed herself to before. She'd even quit her second job at the pancake house across town despite the hole it would mean in her income, and she found she looked forward to coming to work, chatting with the others, talking to the customers. And instead of knocking off directly at closing time, she more often than not lingered on, doing work that could be left to morning, so she could prolong her contact with Renae, brainstorming ideas for new products and displays and services.

And she'd been immensely thankful that although Renae seemed to sense something was wrong, she hadn't said anything.

Until now. Until this morning.

"Renae, I think I've screwed up the best thing that's ever happened to me because of a past I haven't been able to get over."

Lucky thought she should feel surprised that she'd revealed something of such a deeply personal nature, but she didn't. And she wasn't shocked, either, when Renae didn't blink at her, change the subject or turn the other way.

"Pretty screwed-up childhood, huh?"

Renae's words, however, did shock her.

She didn't know what to say so she said nothing.

Renae smiled. "Lucky, I can spot another damaged soul at fifty paces. It's part of the reason I hired you without any solid previous retail experience." She glanced at a car pulling up into a space in front of the store next door. "We lost souls have to look out for each other, you know?"

Lucky felt such a burst of gratitude and warmth toward the other woman she was incapable of speech.

Renae turned her gaze back on her. "You mind if I share a bit of advice I learned a little while ago?"

Lucky stared at her, unsure if she wanted to hear what her friend had to say. "Please," she managed to squeeze out of her tight throat, her hands clutching the cloth.

"You know all the bad stuff you have no control over when you're a kid? I believe that anything that happens before you're eighteen, you're a victim of.'' She seemed to search Lucky's face, as if checking to see if she was really listening. ''Everything that happens after that? Well, it makes you a volunteer.'' She seemed to reflect on something Lucky wasn't privy to, then said, ''Hell, girl, we're all screwed up in some way or another as a result of our childhoods. All you have to do is look at the guys who drink at the strip joint down the way—and the girls who strip there—for an easy example. It's what you do after you grow up that separates those who can take the experience and use it to make them stronger from those who allow the tragedies to destroy them.''

Words so easily said. And so difficult to implement. ''How do you do that? How do you use them to make you stronger?''

''How?'' Renae asked, moving toward her and gently grasping her arms. She turned her to face the lot and the world beyond. ''By looking forward.''

''And forgetting the past?''

Renae briefly tightened the arm over her shoulders. ''No. By accepting it. By knowing it's there and there's nothing you can do to change it, but acknowledging that it doesn't hold power over you anymore. That you are in charge of your life, your future. By moving forward, step by step, breath by breath.''

Lucky's gratitude toward the woman next to her ballooned exponentially.

She lifted her arm, linking it around Renae's slender waist, touching her in a way that she hadn't touched another woman since her mother had died. Then she stared out at the future Renae painted. A future that she was determined to look forward to with a new mind-set and a full heart.

COLIN CONSIDERED the day of work he'd put in so far and felt oddly good about what he'd done. While he didn't expect changes overnight, recognizing that things had to change, that he had to change, was enough for now. As long as he knew there was more work to be done tomorrow.

He glanced at his watch. His couples session with the Hansens was set to begin in five minutes. They'd cancelled their appointment last Monday, and requested to move their weekly sessions to Friday. Something Colin didn't have a problem with.

He leaned forward in his chair and opened their case file. He was disappointed to discover his notes on their sessions were so sparse, horrified to find that he'd passed judgment on them during their first meeting and hadn't done anything really to help them since.

He pulled a fresh notepad form his drawer and began writing.

He was still writing when Jocelyn and Larry Hansen entered and started to take the seats across the room where Colin usually accepted his patients.

Instead he motioned them to sit in the two chairs positioned in front of his desk.

He'd come to the realization today that sitting face to face in a more relaxed environment was preferable when dealing one on one with a single patient. But in the case of couples and groups, sitting close to them, becoming one of them, made it too easy to take on the group mentality, too tempting to tune out.

Also the participants looked upon him as one of them and it was easy for them to disregard his advice and guidance.

Sitting across a desk from them in a position of authority, much like a teacher with students, created a more serious atmosphere.

He noticed the changes in Jocelyn and Larry immediately. Usually Jocelyn would already be tearing her husband down, telling him she'd been waiting all week to tell Colin something, and thus launch into the Jocelyn hour, dominating the conversation and the session.

Now she was uncharacteristically quiet, and she had her feet crossed at the ankles and her hands clasped in her lap, much like a child sent to the principal's office.

Colin made a few more notes, then he put his pen down on top of the pad.

"Larry," he said, sitting back in his chair. "Do you love your wife?"

There was a heartbeat of silence while Colin waited for an answer. He knew it was risky, asking a question this personal. Normally he would be inquiring about what progress and setbacks the couples had experienced over the seven days since their last session.

But he'd decided that remaining impersonal in what were very personal cases wasn't going to get him—or the Hansens—anywhere.

"Of…course I do," Larry finally uttered after looking back and forth between Colin and his wife several times.

Colin nodded, giving a mental sigh of relief. The session would have gone very differently indeed if Larry had answered in the negative.

"When's the last time you told her?"

Silence. Larry didn't appear to know what to say, and Colin wasn't going to help him out.

"He tells me every day," Jocelyn said.

Colin looked at her. "I don't mean at the end of a brief phone call when you two aren't together and you're distracted." He glanced back at Larry. "I'm talking about when you're both at home, perhaps the kids are in bed, and it's just the two of you. Maybe you're sitting in front of the television and you look at your wife and remember the first time you ever set eyes on her. Or think about that moment when you realized this was the woman for you out of all the other women in the world, the one that you wanted to spend the rest of your life with, the one you wanted to create a family with."

Larry blinked at him and Jocelyn's silence spoke volumes.

"I don't know."

"Would you agree it's been a long time?" Colin prompted.

Larry nodded. "Yes. Yes, I would agree."

The other man seemed to look at his wife in a way that didn't speak of frustration or impatience or exasperation. Rather he appeared to be remembering exactly what Colin had asked him to remember.

And Jocelyn's open, questioning expression in response made even Colin sit up and take notice.

"No," Colin said, writing something down on his notepad. "I don't want you to tell her now, Larry."

"Why not?" Jocelyn wanted to know.

Colin held his hand up and smiled. "Because it wouldn't count. Instead, Larry, I want you to remember this moment. I want you to think about it throughout today, into tomorrow and over the next week. And then, when you're really feeling it, you know, when it seems even your toes are bursting with the love you feel for this woman, your wife, I want you to tell her. Then and only then."

In the reflective silence that followed his suggestion, Colin considered that maybe Lucky's secret wasn't what had precipitated this change in him; perhaps his love for Lucky was the true catalyst. Because in order to understand love you had to experience it.

And at that moment he felt he understood it completely.

16

THE SATURDAY-MORNING sunshine spotlighted Colin as he sat on his living-room sofa going over the materials private investigator Jenny Mathena had couriered over to him that morning. Following his last visit with his attorney, he'd decided that he could no longer wait to see what Jamie Polson would do next. He had to take action. He had to protect himself and Lucky from Jamie's escalating obsession with him.

And Jenny Mathena had provided him with the means to do so.

He sat back, thumbing through the photos she'd provided. She'd had one of her people cover Lucky, as well. Colin's eyes lingered on a shot of her standing outside Women Only, her gaze far away. As far away as she was from him right now. As far away as she'd always been from him…and from herself.

He traced his finger down the side of her hauntingly beautiful face, wondering if there would ever be a time he could approach her again. Wondering if she'd welcome him if she saw him at her door or if she'd turn him away.

Had she grouped him with the clutter of men that littered her past? Was she even now using their sad parting as another reason to barricade herself from the world, to continue on being an unhappy soul?

He yearned for her so intensely it was a physical, constant ache. Not merely in his chest, but his stomach. He hadn't known what love was until she'd unwittingly shown him.

It seemed ironical, then, that she would turn that love away when he revealed it.

Colin put the photograph down with the others and closed his eyes, missing Lucky with every molecule of his being.

Lucky…

It seemed incongruous to him that someone named Lucky should have had such an unlucky life. But what remained was that while he could see her pain, analyze it, he could never truly understand it. Know what it was like to have lived in her shoes.

What he did understand was that until she was ready to open up, to seek help with her journey, he was helpless to do anything but stand back and watch her let the bitter sadness of her past destroy her. Destroy any chance they had for a future.

Destroy their love.

He glanced at his watch. He'd contacted the housemother at Crossroads and asked if it was possible for him to stop by and visit Melissa. She'd been surprised by his call, but welcomed his visit. It meant forgoing his weekly tennis match with Will, but he felt this was more important to him right now. More important to him and to Melissa.

Besides, Will had his own problems to work out now with his young resident and the impasse they'd reached in their sex life. Colin couldn't begin to help him with those problems.

He slid the photographs and the information back into the envelope in which there'd been delivered, then grabbed the small bag of items he'd bought for Melissa—the latest best-selling young adult novel, cosmetics designed to make any girl her age feel pretty, and a small, white stuffed bear wearing a T-shirt that said Princess. Personal items she'd unfairly never gotten and that he wanted to help her start to re-accumulate, if just to learn they weren't important in the overall scheme of things.

No, he might not be able to help Lucky and, by extension, them as a couple.

But maybe he would be just in time to help Melissa.

THE ONLY sounds in Lucky's apartment that night came from the small transistor radio tuned to her favorite oldies station—the tinny rendition of ''Sitting on the Dock of the Bay'' seemed to characterize the hot, humid June night—and the cadence of crickets outside her open window. Around her the meager items that constituted the whole of her life were packed away into bags and boxes, ready to move, although she didn't know where she would be moving to yet.

Lucky sat at the chipped linoleum-covered table, a single box the size of a crate in front of her. She hadn't opened the box in over five years, but it had moved with her from place to place, apartment to apartment, the first thing in, the last thing out when she came and went. She slowly moved her hands over the top and sides, considering what it held, the significance of what she was about to do. The box and its contents represented the past that she'd left behind. The box was the last bruise against her heart.

She took a deep breath and lifted the top, allowing it to slide off to the side. She didn't realize she'd closed her eyes until she opened them to stare at the contents within.

The first thing that caught her eye was a small pillow covered in eyelet lace that was as familiar to her as her own reflection. Her mother had made it for her when she was five and she had had a hand in decorating her room for the first time. Every morning when she'd made her bed it had been the last thing she'd put on top. Every night before she'd gone to bed, it had been the first thing she'd taken off.

The ghost of a smile played along her lips as she lifted the heart-shaped pillow to her face then pressed it to her nose, breathing in the scent of lavender and rosemary, the smells of her childhood, flooding her mind with happy memories of her mother, of her family, before everything fell apart.

It had been so long since she'd thought about that time in her life. The laughter, the holiday meals, so many milestones that she'd blocked out in favor of clutching the blackness that had fallen over her.

Was Renae right? Was she now a volunteer rather than a victim? Was she to blame for the stark state of her life, holding on to old hurts when she might have been able to move beyond them?

It seemed improbable, but not impossible.

More and more she seemed to be open to other ideas, to be willing to take a look at her life from a different direction. And while nothing had been capable of erasing the pain she'd felt almost every day for the past sixteen years, she no longer winced away from it.

Lucky put the pillow in her lap then reached in for the next item. The eight-by-ten frame was cheap, but the degree in business in her name it held wasn't.

Right behind the frame was a savings passbook. Still holding the frame, she opened the check-sized plastic holder. The bulk of the money she'd inherited upon her father's death was still there, the only withdrawals had been to cover her college tuition. She hadn't even relied on the money to pay for room and board but had instead worked throughout college to support herself, the money seeming tainted somehow. The degree she'd used the money to achieve had seemed dirtied, as well.

She'd wished for her father's death and he had died. Which made her reluctance to touch anything connected to her inheritance doubly intense.

The next item in the box was the family photo album.

She paused, not knowing if she was up to opening it. She smoothed her fingers over the faded, dark leather. She hadn't looked at it since the day of her mother's funeral. She had been unable to gaze at the other life she had once known, for it made what had come after doubly painful.

Now she opened it, the smell of old paper and photographs filling her senses.

The pages were filled with memories her mother had so carefully catalogued of smiling faces, her first steps, her first bike…and the three of them as a family.

She caught herself staring at her father's face, back then happy and handsome and full of the right kind of love for her.

Accept…move forward.

Renae's words echoed in her mind. She'd lived so long with one foot firmly planted in the dark shadow of her teenage years that she didn't know how to pull it out. But she vowed that she would learn. And she would not only bring the foot parallel with the other, she would edge it forward, finally taking a step toward the future.

She would one day be able to look at the past

and not feel as though it had happened yesterday. Would remember the good along with the bad.

She closed the album and hugged it to her chest, a mental photograph of another man filling her mind and her heart.

Colin…

Her heart gave a tender squeeze.

As for Colin, he deserved better than what she could give him just then. He deserved more than the shattered soul she had to offer.

And she vowed one day to give it to him if he'd still have her.

COLIN STOOD at the double doors to the mammoth house that bore the address in the file Jenny Mathena had given him. He'd wanted to come earlier, but his brief visit with Melissa had turned into a day-long event at Crossroads, ending in him sticking around for dinner with the house mates on the premises and Kathy Oberon, the housemother. He'd even kicked in with clean-up.

When he'd finally left a half hour ago, Kathy had thanked him for coming, for helping the teens.

He'd told her that they were helping him more than he could ever help them. And after spending casual time in their company, drinking in their unflappable spirit, that's exactly the way he felt.

While he'd gotten to know them to a certain degree during the group sessions he'd sat in on monthly, he'd never seen their other sides. He'd marveled at how...normal they'd appeared. They'd looked and acted just like the houseful of teenagers that they were. While he'd read about the resiliency of the human spirit, he had never viewed it firsthand.

Today, he had.

And that gave him even more hope for what he was about to do.

Clutching the envelope from the private investigator under his left arm, he knocked on the door in front of him with his right.

Jamie Polson, aka James Randolph Polson, IV. Only son of wealthy Toledo industrialist James Randolph Polson, III. Twenty-nine years of age, unemployed, five years of college with a degree in nothing.

And another member of the walking wounded Colin was beginning to realize comprised a good deal of the regular population.

The door opened on a housekeeper who blinked at him before saying, "May I help you?"

"Yes. I'd like to speak with Jamie, please."

"Is he expecting you?"

No, Colin thought. He probably wasn't.

But he should be.

"Yes," he lied.

The housekeeper led him into what looked like a library, replete with floor-to-ceiling bookcases. Everywhere he looked reeked of money and privilege.

Everywhere he looked reeked of isolation and loneliness.

He knew this was Jamie's father's house. And that James Randall Polson, III, for all intents and purposes didn't live there anymore, but rather home was his Myrtle Beach estate home where he lived with his fourth wife, a woman half his age.

Jamie lived all by himself in this hulking, dark manor, with nothing but the staff to keep him company.

It occurred to Colin that perhaps in some patients' cases a house visit would be in order. In two minutes he'd learned more about Jamie than in six months of one-on-one sessions.

Of course, having a private investigator look into a patient's past was bad form, and was very likely illegal. But Jamie had crossed the line from patient months ago and there was no turning back.

Except for this one last session.

"What are you doing here?"

Colin slowly turned to face Jamie where he stood in the open doorway. Though the same height as Colin, Jamie had a much thinner frame, the polo shirt and shorts he wore ill-fitting, too big, as if they weren't his clothes at all but somebody else's.

His father's?

"I've come to convince you to call this whole thing to a halt."

Jamie lifted a brow. "Why ever would I want to do that?"

Colin had been afraid he'd say that. And was prepared for it.

"Why did you never tell me you were homosexual?" Colin asked, rather than answering Jamie's question.

Jamie's grin was one-hundred-percent malevolent. "Well, Dr. McKenna, why do you think my father, the king of heterosexual males, runs a tab with nearly every shrink in town? Because I'm straight?"

"Then I think your father might be interested in learning that his gay son bedded his young stepmother on the chaise lounge in their backyard in Myrtle Beach a little over a year ago."

Jamie appeared prepared to deny the charges, but Colin held up the envelope in his hands to stop him. He didn't need to show the proof. Just knowing he had it was enough for him. And apparently for Jamie.

"What better way to prove to dear old dad that you're not gay?" Jamie said quietly, the bitter challenge in his voice gone.

"But once you did it you couldn't bring yourself to confront your father with it, could you?"

Jamie didn't say anything, merely stared at him as if he'd like nothing more in that moment than to see him gone. "*Now* you play therapist. Isn't that special?"

Colin mentally winced but kept himself from visibly reacting, Jamie's comment hit a little too close to home. "If you'll remember, I suggested you consult with someone else because it was obvious we were just wasting each other's time."

Jamie's smile was nothing short of malicious. "I'd have loved to have seen your face when you were served the initial intent to sue papers."

Colin narrowed his eyes. Even after everything that had happened, all that Jamie had done, he'd been woefully unprepared for the malice dripping from the other man's voice. "My guess is that if you didn't see my face, you had someone get a picture of it for you.''

Jamie didn't say anything.

''Is that how you occupy your time nowadays, Jamie? No dad around to bully and poke for a reaction, so you've transferred your immature, juvenile play for attention on to others.''

''You don't know anything about me.''

''On the contrary, Jamie, I think I know more than even you know about yourself.''

He put the series of photos on the nearby desk.

''I stopped by to see if we could work this out, Jamie. Despite everything, I don't want to add more hurt to what you've already experienced from other people in your life.'' He shook his head. ''But since that's not going to happen, I thought I'd let you know that I'm planning on leveling the playing field a little. In that envelope you'll not only find shots of you taking liberties with your father's wife, you'll find photos of you gaining access to my apartment, following me around. I'd have to check with my attorney, but I'm pretty sure what you've been doing falls solidly into stalker category.''

Jamie stood completely still, apparently unsure what to do now that his bluff had been called.

''So know that if you continue to pursue this

fraudulent case against me, I'm going to counter-sue for libel. And given your past record of bringing false suits against a number of others…well, guess who the courts and Daddy are going to believe?''

Colin stepped toward the hall, but before he left he stopped alongside Jamie and said, ''My advice to you would be to get out of this house…now. The sooner the better. You need to get out there and find out what life is really about, kid. Accept your homosexuality, embrace it even, and push aside whatever issues remain between you and your dad until after you get to know yourself a little better. Learn to support yourself. See that there's more to life than trying to make everybody else's as miserable as yours.''

Jamie had kept his gaze forward and Colin watched as he swallowed hard.

Colin softened his voice. ''And if you want a referral to a good therapist who just might be able to help you if you let her, here's her card.''

When Jamie didn't reach out for it, Colin slid it into the other man's breast pocket.

He crossed the cavernous foyer, opened the door, then looked back to see Jamie holding the card and reading it.

17

THE LETTER was delivered in care of Women Only.

Lucky stood at the counter and froze midway through sorting the mail. In the upper left-hand corner of the plain white envelope Colin had written his name and address.

Her heart did a triple beat as she turned away from Renae.

"I'm going to go straighten up in back," Lucky whispered, unsure if Renae had heard her but too preoccupied to care. She walked into the massage therapy room and pulled the curtain shut behind her, unaware that it was still half open as she stared at the envelope she held.

Shakily, she tore open the end.

Inside was a simple square sheet of personal notepaper.

Meet me at this address on Thursday at 7:00 p.m.

It was signed simply Colin.

She absently pushed her hair back from her face as she turned the paper over then back again, rereading the words. The address, though near downtown, wasn't that of his apartment. She didn't recognize it at all.

''What is it?''

Lucky looked up to find Renae watching her through the partially open curtain. ''Um, nothing. Colin wants me to meet him somewhere.''

Renae came to stand next to her, reading the note over her shoulder. Such familiarity would have made Lucky bristle a week or so ago. Now she welcomed it as she tilted the note so Renae could read it.

''Cryptic. Are you going to go?''

Lucky swallowed thickly. ''I don't know.''

She felt Renae's hand on her shoulder. ''If you go, you don't have to stay, you know that, don't you?''

Lucky nodded.

''But even I'm curious to see what the sexy doc has up his sleeve.''

Lucky stared at her. ''How did you know he was a doctor?''

Renae shrugged and smiled at her. ''When I

first saw him come in here I knew I'd recognized him from somewhere. His friend owns the condo downstairs from mine.''

"Will?''

"You know him?''

"We've met once or twice.''

"Now talk about your sexy docs. I wouldn't mind getting the tongue depressors and anal thermometers out for that one.''

Lucky burst out laughing, recognizing the sound of happiness in her own voice.

"Now that's something I haven't heard in a while,'' Renae remarked. "I think you should go, Lucky. Hear what he has to say.''

"I don't know if I'm ready yet.''

"Sweetie, if any of us waited for when we were ready, well, we'd be waiting forever.''

COLIN COULDN'T REMEMBER a time when he'd been more nervous. He paced the floor in front of the door to Crossroads, pushing his watch around his wrist and staring out the front window at any cars that might be entering the parking lot.

It was five after seven and upstairs the group was already gathering, waiting for him to join them before beginning the rap session.

He absently rubbed the back of his neck. He hadn't really considered what he'd do if Lucky didn't come. Sure, he'd realized the possibility existed, but once he'd put his plans in motion he'd moved full steam ahead, not allowing for variations.

Such as her not showing.

Damn.

He stared at the face of his watch again, trying to work out a cut-off point. If she didn't show within the next five minutes, he'd have to admit that she probably wasn't going to show.

The door beside him opened, startling him. He looked up to find Lucky standing there, her vivid green eyes wide, her face pale.

''Hi,'' he said, silently cursing himself for the lame greeting. But he couldn't help himself. It seemed a lifetime since he'd last seen her, heard her voice, enjoyed being in her presence. And just looking at her made his longing for her multiply exponentially.

''Hi, yourself.'' She offered up a shaky smile. ''What is this place?''

His plan. Standing there gaping at her, Colin had nearly forgotten where they were and what he'd planned to do.

''I'm glad you came,'' he said quietly.

She searched his eyes for a long moment. "I'm glad I came, too."

He held out his hand for hers, hoping that he was doing the right thing. Praying that he wasn't rushing things. But he'd sensed on a fundamental level that calling her up and asking her out on a date wouldn't have brought her to him. So he'd determined that while he couldn't help her, he could maybe help her to help herself.

"They're waiting for us," he said.

She slowly looked around the quiet first floor of the old house, craning her neck to peer into the rooms branching off from the foyer.

"This is a shelter," he said as he began leading her up the narrow staircase.

"A shelter? For whom? Homeless people?" A shadow of wariness backlit her eyes.

"Of a sort, yes," he said, purposely being cagey.

He was afraid if she knew it was a shelter for runaway teens she'd turn and walk straight out the door.

His hope was that the instant she saw the kids face to face, she wouldn't be able to turn away. Just as he hadn't been able to so many years before.

"Everybody, I'd like you to meet Lucky," Colin said as he drew her into the room.

"Hi, Lucky," the eighteen teenagers greeted loudly.

LUCKY FELT like the section of wooden flooring she was standing on had just been cut out from under her.

A shelter…the age of the kids in the room… She realized that the house wasn't a place for homeless adults, but homeless children. Children the same age she'd been when she'd needed help. When she'd run away.

Her hand felt ice-cold in Colin's warm grasp. She was helpless to do anything but follow as he led her to a loveseat grouped in with the other sofas and chairs. She sat down, her legs feeling as substantial as water.

Why had Colin invited her there? She looked at him, her heart pounding in her chest.

As a woman slightly older than her on the other side of the room directed the teenagers to introduce and tell a little about themselves, he seemed to tune into her need to know more. "I volunteer here," Colin whispered to her. "And I thought it was something you might like to see."

Across from her, a girl of about thirteen began

speaking, and Lucky's gaze riveted on her young face. Miranda. Her alcoholic mother had abandoned her when she was ten, her father had left her home by herself most of the time, and she'd been a full-fledged alcoholic and drug user by age eleven.

Lucky's chest felt so tight she nearly couldn't breathe.

"My name's Jason," the teenage boy next to Miranda said. "I'm sixteen, have been through twenty homes in the foster-care system since I was five, and I...I tried to commit suicide last month."

Lucky's gaze dropped to where red, puckered scars were plainly visible on his wrists.

She tried to tug her hand from Colin's, but he held tight.

The next teen spoke. Then the next. And with each, Lucky felt both overwhelmed and awed. Not only by what they had endured and were continuing to endure, but by the calm, reflective way they were able to tell their stories. A couple of them ended their introductions with "and I'm going to be all right." And she couldn't help believing that with the faith and friendship they were surrounded by they would not only be all right, they would flourish.

What had Renae called her? A damaged soul.

Every last one of these teens was a damaged soul. And though she'd once closed off her heart in order to deal with her own past, now it opened up so wide it seemed impossible to stop the love that poured out.

She realized it was Colin's turn to speak and she turned to look at him, her gaze feasting on everything that was him.

"I'm Dr. Colin McKenna and I've been volunteering here at Crossroads for the past three years. I've seen many teens come and go, some onto better things, some to seek out the rock bottom they need to hit in order to make the journey back. But this group here…this group has to be the most impressive yet."

The teens laughed.

"On a more serious note…"

Lucky blinked when he looked at her.

"I used to fool myself into thinking I was doing a good deed by coming here once a month. It made me sleep a little easier at night knowing I was doing something. Until I realized that I didn't have a clue as to what was truly going on, and that my efforts didn't amount to a drop in the bucket compared to what I could be doing. So now I'm here two to three times a week for however long I'm needed." He quietly cleared his throat. ''And I'm always shocked to discover that I learn more from each of you about love and life and the beauty of the human spirit than I could ever teach you.''

Hot tears burned Lucky's eyes as she searched his handsome face. Whereas he'd been merely sexy before, a man she could spend the rest of her life looking at and never tire of his features, now he emerged so breathtakingly beautiful she was spellbound.

After long moments she became aware of the silence in the room around her. She glanced at the participants, finding them looking at her warmly.

She realized they were waiting for her to speak.

Panic rose up from her stomach and she searched her mind for some wise-ass crack to make, something that would diffuse the somber atmosphere in the room, deflect the attention away from her.

Instead she squeezed Colin's hand and said, ''Hi, my name's Lucky Clayborn. And I'm going to be all right.''

And in that one moment she knew that she would be.

''IT WAS NICE MEETING YOU,'' the last of the teens said to Lucky at the door. ''Come back and visit anytime.''

Her answer was a smile as she returned a hug, her gaze glued to Colin's face over the girl's shoulder.

Colin shifted his feet. While it appeared that Lucky had responded well to his surprise, he knew that he couldn't fully know what was going on inside her mind, inside her heart. All he knew was that he'd had to try to help her move on somehow, and regular therapy sessions weren't doing it for her. She'd thrown up a giant road-block the first time she'd come to her session with him. And he understood from his partner that she wasn't having much luck making any major breakthroughs with her, either.

So he'd thought that if he approached from a reversion-type position, put her in a room with kids the age she had been when she'd gone through what she had, he might be able to reach her somehow.

And his heart had contracted when he'd seen her connect with the kids, seeming to have gained some sort of acceptance about her situation. He didn't kid himself into thinking he was responsible for it. But he'd like to think he'd played a small role in her progress.

He'd liked to think he could continue playing a larger role in her life.

Finally they were alone. Or as alone as two people could get with so many teenagers in one house. Sounds of laughter came from the kitchen. The television was on in the room to their right. And upstairs a girl was upset that someone had borrowed her shirt without telling her.

But all Colin could see was Lucky.

She avoided his gaze and quietly cleared her throat. "They're a great bunch of kids."

"That they are."

She lifted her face to look at him, her eyes filled with curiosity. "Thank you for inviting me."

He nodded. "Thanks for coming."

Colin wanted to invite her out. Offer to drive her home. Ask her to come back to his place with him. But he knew it was too soon for any of that. He'd already decided that he wasn't going to pursue anything more with her. Not now. Not tonight. His invitation had been but the first of many steps he had planned to work Lucky back into his life. Not just now, but forever.

She appeared uncomfortable. "Um, I guess I'll be going now."

Colin nodded again, thrusting his hands deep into his pants pockets to keep from reaching out for her. Touching her. "Good night."

She looked a little confused and his resolve nearly snapped. Then she turned and with a final wave to the teens looking on from the other room, she walked out the door.

18

COLIN HAD NEVER KNOWN a week could be so long. Seven days that seemed a lifetime, simply because he'd gone that time without seeing Lucky. He hadn't feasted on her lovely face, looked into her remarkable eyes, kissed her lush, provocative lips.

But if his plan had a chance in hell of working, he'd have to take things one slow step at a time. And if he needed any reminder of that, the fact that Lucky hadn't tried to contact him since the Crossroads session shouted it at him.

One good thing happening in his life just then was that ever since his visit to Jamie, he hadn't received any peculiar notes or threats or suffered any damage to his property. And private investigator Jenny Mathena assured him that nothing was being done to Lucky, either. Which, of course, might have something to do with Colin's no longer seeing her.

He sat back in his office chair, making a few

final notes on the addictive personality session
he'd just led, then closed the file. He was easily
doing double the work he had before, but curiously his activity seemed to fill him with twice
the energy rather than draining his emotional and
physical resources. He still jogged every morning,
but no longer maintained the punishing pace he'd
set for himself before.

Of course, life would be a whole hell of a lot
easier if Will could have some luck in his efforts
to bed the young resident he'd been dating. What
had been weekly tennis matches were now twice
a week, only because Colin didn't have time for
more due to his commitment to Crossroads and
his plan to win back Lucky.

Anyway, he didn't think he could handle the
brutal matches into which Will channeled all of
his sexual frustration more than twice a week. He
was even toying with the idea of buying his friend
an inflatable "date," his argument being that if
the girl wasn't real it wasn't really cheating.

The telephone at his elbow rang and he picked
it up after the first ring.

"Mr. Maddox on the line for you, Dr. Mc-
Kenna," Annette said.

He thanked the secretary as he scratched the
back of his neck. What could Don want? He gri-

maced, hoping it wasn't bad news. Maybe he'd pushed Jamie straight into filing official charges against him with the county prosecutor's office.

"Colin!" Don Maddox's voice boomed over the receiver. "Good news, buddy. James Randolph Polson, IV, dropped the case."

Colin's relief was immediate and complete. "I can't tell you how glad I am to hear that."

"Not any happier than I am, dear boy. Not any happier than I am. This whole debacle had the makings of a real mess."

He was telling him. "What happens if Jamie wakes up tomorrow and changes his mind?"

"Thankfully, the chances of that are slim to none. Polson's attorney, whom I also happen to golf with once a week at Inverness, tells me James is in the process of moving to San Francisco where he's going to open an art gallery."

Colin smiled. *Good for you, Jamie. Good for you.* "I'm happy to hear it."

And he was. Because it might mean that Jamie would stop taking his misery out on others and start concentrating on making himself happy.

Don sighed. "I won't keep you. I just thought you'd want to hear the news the instant I got it."

"Thanks, Don. It's very good news indeed."

He slowly replaced the receiver then got up and

went to the filing cabinets behind him. Opening the one marked *P* he thumbed through the files until he found Jamie's, stamped Closed across it with the stamp in his middle desk drawer, then put the file in his out box for Annette to put away in the archives.

Then he grabbed his jacket and headed out the back way, his only thought to get home and continuing his plans for winning back Lucky.

TRAFFIC WAS LIGHT and the weather was perfect, making the drive from Sylvania to downtown Toledo almost a pleasure rather than a trial of patience. Colin parked his car on the street, relieved that he no longer had anything to worry about in that regard, then took the elevator upstairs and unlocked his door.

The instant he entered his apartment, he noticed something different.

He stood stock-still for a long moment, trying to put his finger on it. Then he identified the difference. Not so much a difference, really, but an addition. A scent. More specifically the smell of ginger, the scent Lucky always wore.

His heart pitched to sit on the marble floor next to his feet.

Of course, he knew she still had his key. And

secretly he was glad she hadn't felt the need to return it. As for her using it, he hadn't dared to entertain such high hopes.

He put down his keys and his jacket and walked into the kitchen to find everything exactly the way he'd left it, and then he crossed the living room to the master suite where, again, everything was in order.

Then he spotted it. The piece of white notepaper in the middle of the coffee table…along with a single key.

His stomach clenched so tightly he nearly doubled over with the pain of it.

She had returned his key.

He slowly crossed the living room toward the table, hardly daring to hope he was wrong. Praying he was seeing things. But he wasn't.

He slid the folded note out from under the key then opened it.

> Dear Colin—I figure it's only fair.
> Meet me at…

He went on to read an unfamiliar address in the nearby Old West End section of Toledo.

He reached down to pick up the key. It was then he realized that it wasn't his key.

LUCKY STOOD IN THE KITCHEN of her new one-bedroom apartment—easily four times the size of her old apartment—and forced herself to stop looking at the clock every two seconds. Colin would come.

Wouldn't he?

She burned herself as she took lasagna from the oven, waving her hand to cool it before sticking it under cold running water. Ever since she'd seen him last week she'd known it was time to invite him back in. When she'd gazed into his eyes right before she'd left Crossroads, she'd known down to her bones that she loved the man, and that he not only loved her, he…well, he got her. He'd obviously done some soul-searching of his own while they'd been apart and it looked good on him.

Good? It had been all she could do not to use her key to his place that first night.

But considering all she'd gone through already that night, and on so many nights before and since, she'd thought it a good idea to take things a little slower. For a decade she'd rushed into relationships then just as quickly rushed back out.

But this one…Colin…well, he deserved special consideration. And not just because she owed him.

And she did owe him. More than any human being on the face of the earth. That night on his balcony he'd forced her not only to share the ghosts of her past but face them down. And while initially she'd hated him for it, she was coming to see that the showdown was long overdue. She'd wasted too many years living in self-imposed isolation. She'd lived in squalor because she couldn't bring herself to touch money that was rightfully hers. Couldn't bring herself to use her education because to do so would require more commitment than she'd been prepared to give to any job.

She'd begun meeting Dr. Morgan Szymanski for one-on-one sessions instead of group sessions this past week. And during the very first appointment Morgan had helped her realize that all these years she'd blamed herself for her father's behavior. That maybe if she'd dressed differently, acted differently, she could have made him not want her. Morgan had helped her understand that while nothing could excuse her father's behavior, it was well documented that after a family tragedy—such as the death of her mother, the anchor of their family—the male parent often mixed up familial roles. It didn't mean he hadn't loved her as his daughter. But without help and intervention, his mental illness had worsened until he'd believed the only just punishment for his actions was taking his own life.

Lucky didn't kid herself into thinking she was all right. But she did take comfort in the belief that one day she would be, just as she'd told the kids at Crossroads.

Not only had she moved from her dilapidated apartment into this larger, airier one in the charming older section of Toledo, she'd put together a proposal for Renae to open another satellite shop of Women Only downtown, using her inheritance to fund the project. Renae had been ecstatic with the prospect and they were already shopping for a home for the new place.

Still with everything she'd been doing lately, she realized one thing was glaringly missing. Or rather someone: Colin.

Merely thinking about him made her heart beat faster and her palms dampen.

Dear, sweet, sexy Colin.

She turned to put the dish of lasagna on the old oak table she'd positioned in the middle of the kitchen and spotted him standing in the kitchen doorway. She didn't know how long he'd been there, but she suspected it was a while, given his relaxed stance and the way he leaned against the jamb.

Her mouth watered with the intense desire to kiss him.

Her heart squeezed with the intense desire to love him.

"Hi," she said, giving him what could only be classified as a goofy smile.

"Hi, yourself." His smile made her toes curl inside her sandals.

Though he had never been inside the new place, it felt as if he'd been there forever. It felt as if he belonged there. They belonged there. Together.

Then again, it really didn't matter where he was, or she was. So long as they were there together.

"I have to warn you up front. I need to take this slow," she said.

He nodded, his dark eyes serious. "We'll go as slow as you like."

She realized she still held the lasagna dish and put it down in the middle of the table. With shaking hands, she took off her oven mitts.

Then, before she knew that's what she was going to do, she rushed to the opposite side of the room and threw herself into Colin's arms, her fingers bunching into his thick, soft hair, her mouth finding his cheek…and his eyebrow…and his forehead…then finally his mouth.

Oh, how she'd missed this. How she'd missed him. He made her feel beautiful and special and safe and loved. He made her feel like there wasn't a thing in the world she couldn't do if she put her mind to it. And that was a very precious gift, indeed.

Morgan had told her that she'd need to retrain herself sexually. That jumping into bed was never a good idea. But already Lucky realized a difference in her physical reaction to Colin. Yes, she wanted him with a desperation that took her breath away. But she also felt her heart swell in her chest. She felt the warmth of love swirl through her veins, the sense of completeness, of coming home that came with merely being in his arms.

And surely that couldn't be wrong.

Reluctantly, she hauled her mouth away, then rested her forehead against his, laughing into his eyes.

"Is that your idea of slow?" he asked, his voice thick with desire, his eyes brimming with love.

"I think it's a better idea if we maybe make things up as we go along," she whispered.

"That's the best idea I've heard in a long, long time.…"

Epilogue

One month later…

COLIN FOUND IT IMPOSSIBLE to believe that just a short time ago he'd had to run to combat his sexual frustration. Now he was running to keep up his stamina so that he could keep up with Lucky, both in and out of the bedroom.

His feet slapped against the cement path through Promenade Park, the Maumee River catching the first rays of the rising summer sun. It never ceased to amaze him how everything looked the same. He'd undergone so many changes in the past couple of months that surely the world around him should have changed as well.

Instead the summer grew hotter. The days grew longer.

And his love for Lucky grew more and more.

"You're a sadist," she said beside him, her

tennis shoes having a difficult time keeping up with his.

Colin slowed the pace, reminding himself that she wasn't used to running. At least not physically. Emotionally…well, she'd done enough of that to last a lifetime.

He drew to a stop, watching as she doubled over, trying to catch her breath.

He grinned at her. ''You're not supposed to do that.''

Her damp red ponytail shifted to the side of her face as she considered him from the corner of her eyes. ''It works for me.''

He shook his head and stepped to the railing overlooking the muddy depths of the Maumee. Moments later she stepped next to him, automatically tucking her hand inside his. Colin marveled at the simple yet meaningful movement as he lifted the back of her hand to his mouth and kissed it. She smiled, then kissed the back of his hand. Then both of them turned to take in the view, their heads together, staring out at a future that promised to be as bright and golden as the sunrise bathing them in its summer warmth.

* * *

Wicked, *Tori Carrington's second title in her* SLEEPING WITH SECRETS *trilogy, is available next month!*

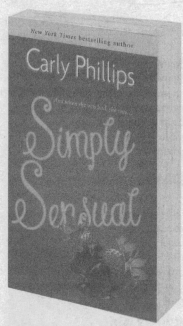

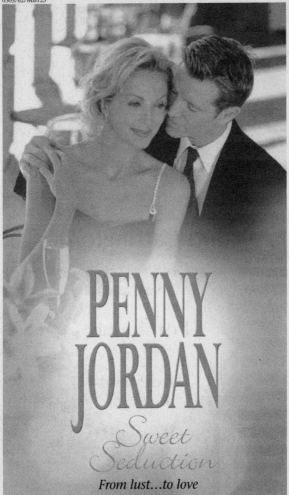

FREE!

2 Books
and a surprise gift!

We would like to take this opportunity to thank you for reading this Mills & Boon® book by offering you the chance to take TWO more specially selected titles from the Blaze™ series absolutely FREE! We're also making this offer to introduce you to the benefits of the Reader Service™—

- ★ FREE home delivery
- ★ FREE gifts and competitions
- ★ FREE monthly Newsletter
- ★ Exclusive Reader Service offers
- ★ Books available before they're in the shops

Accepting these FREE books and gift places you under no obligation to buy, you may cancel at any time, even after receiving your free shipment. Simply complete your details below and return the entire page to the address below. You don't even need a stamp!

YES! Please send me 2 free Blaze books and a surprise gift. I understand that unless you hear from me, I will receive 4 superb new titles every month for just £3.05 each, postage and packing free. I am under no obligation to purchase any books and may cancel my subscription at any time. The free books and gift will be mine to keep in any case.

K5ZEF

Ms/Mrs/Miss/Mr ....Initials ....
BLOCK CAPITALS PLEASE
Surname ....
Address...

....

....Postcode ....

Send this whole page to:
UK: FREEPOST CN81, Croydon, CR9 3WZ